THREE DEADLY TRIALS

Battle for The Dark King | Book One

VS WINTERS

Edited by
CHRISTINE THOMPSON

Chapter One

"WHY DID I AGREE TO THIS?" I GRUMBLED TO MYSELF WHILE slathering a second layer of sheer gloss onto my full lips.

Sliding the applicator back into the tube, I let it fall from my fingertips and onto the vanity so that I could fluff my long, crimson curls. My eyes shifted from the liner, rimming them to my younger sister, Ava, as she flounced through the doorway into my room. With a glance up from her incessant texting, she paused to stare at me with a loose jaw.

"Shut up," I said before the question could leave her mouth.

A grin formed on her lips as she took me in from crown to toe. I twitched in the snug black dress hugging my curves. It revealed a little more cleavage than I would have preferred and hit just above mid-thigh. Not my usual style.

She giggled.

"You're finally doing it. You are going on a date with Benjamin, aren't you?" She stretched out a flawlessly manicured finger and tapped the end of my nose.

"Stop that." I waived her and her ridiculous smile aside.

"I knew this day would come," Ava feigned pride, wiping a tear from her cheek.

"Ava, can you please just--" I sighed and turned back to the mirror to adjust my hair for the hundredth time. It was a nervous habit.

"Here, let me help."

Ava was much more experienced than I was when it came to female beautification techniques. The two hours of effort I had wasted on my hair took her only a matter of minutes to fix. She tidied it into a set of twists and knots at the nape of my neck, strategically leaving delicate wisps to hang loosely, framing my heart-shaped face.

"That's better, no offense. Now, tell me everything." She dropped her perfect little frame onto my mattress and clasped her fists under her chin in anticipation of a story that wasn't coming.

"I only agreed to one drink. Nothing more than that. And it's only to get him off of my back about it."

"Come on, Eden. The guy has been asking for, what, two years? He's practically in love with you. Plus, he is drop-dead gorgeous."

I glared at her reflection. I knew she wasn't wrong, despite my instinctive response. The guy wouldn't leave me alone at the office during work hours. And he was handsome, in a bad-boy kind of way. She rolled her large hazel eyes at me like she always did and flung her bleached ponytail over her shoulder. What a teenager.

"What are your plans for tonight?" I asked, changing the subject from my less than stellar love life.

Ava shrugged and looked back to her phone. It had a glittery pink case, which was just *so* Ava. And, as though I had reminded her of something, she started texting. I continued to glare as her fingernails clacked against the oversized screen.

"Hello? Earth to Ava?"

She glanced up at me but quickly returned to her phone, making me grind my teeth.

"Ava!"

"I was just confirming plans with Ash, chill out. We are going to the theater to catch a movie then hanging out at her place."

"Will you be staying the night?"

"Yeah, probably."

"Fine. But I expect a text or call tonight and another in the morning. What are the rules?"

I turned to face her. Crossing my arms over my chest, I waited for her to relay them.

"I know the rules." She said, matching my pose.

"Then let's hear them."

Ava sighed and stood, pink phone in hand. I was willing to bet it never left her grasp.

"No boys, no drinking, and no running around after curfew."

"And?"

"And if I don't check in with you, I will be grounded until the end of time."

"Great," I smiled and patted her on the head before she could shrink out of reach. "Stay safe and have fun with your friends."

She whined about her hair, but I ignored her and dialed a number on my own cell. The sound of her packing an overnight back echoed through the hall as I made my way to the kitchen. The receiver clicked on, and I straightened my shoulders as though they could see me.

"Ithaca medical center, how can I assist you?" Pleasant words, but the woman sounded annoyed.

"Room 233, please."

She put me through, and I tapped my arm while the appalling elevator music blasted from the other end. A mountain of unpaid bills sat unopened and staring at me as I paced across the kitchen's cream-colored linoleum.

"Hello?" My father's raspy voice cut the music off.

"Hey, Dad," I grabbed my purse and house key.

"Hey hon," He huffed, as though answering the phone had taken every last bit of his energy. It probably had.

"How's Ava? Big plans for the weekend?"

"Oh, you know, just being eighteen. She's hanging out with some friends tonight. How are you doing?"

My father snorted, which sent him into a hacking fit that made me grimace. He didn't like talking about his illness, not that he really had a choice at this point. Before cancer had taken hold, he had been a hard-ass. Tom Morris, the cop, and a damn good one at that. When they had diagnosed him, it took a toll on us as a family, causing splinters that had never really mended.

"I'm doing okay. Doc says we have a long way to go still."

No matter how many times I heard him say that, my heart still sank. The "doc" had also told him he only had a few months left with us. It was a hard thing to wrap my head around, the thought that soon it would be just my angst-filled baby sister and me.

At twenty-one years old, I was only a few years Ava's senior, but it felt like much more than that. Especially since I had been forced to drop out of my first year at college and let my dreams run down the drain to come home and help. She didn't really need it, as she would be graduating next spring, but dad didn't feel right leaving her alone while he was in and out of treatment.

"We will get through Daddy, you're the strongest man I know. I love you, and I'll be by to see you first thing on Sunday, okay?" I waved to Ava as she left through the front door, her friend's car just visible behind her. She waved back and slammed it shut.

"Alright, Eden. Make sure your sister isn't doing anything stupid."

"Always do, Dad. Love you."

I disconnected. My eyes lingered on the screen as it faded to black. I couldn't allow myself to lose control right now. The idea of the date alone had my nerves all up in knots. With a huff, I pulled on my matte black three-inch heels and left through the back door.

A gathering of wispy clouds on the horizon grew rosy as the sun dropped low behind the buildings. The warmth of summer felt pleasant against my fair skin, and I had a passing thought that maybe I should get out of the house more.

I didn't know then that I should have turned around.

That I should have locked myself in and stuffed my face with junk food while watching trash TV.

Perhaps if I had, he would have chosen someone other than me.

Chapter Two

"GOOD TO SEE YOU, EDEN."

Benjamin greeted me with teeth far too white for any regular person to have. He extracted a chair from the table he had been sitting at before I strolled inside, hips swaying. We exchanged an awkward handshake, and he held out an arm to the seat. I accepted the gesture.

"Good to see you as well. Sorry if I'm a little late."

I tucked a stray curl behind my ear and avoided eye contact as he took a seat across from me. The eyes of random strangers observing me along the street made me much less nervous than being under Ben's dark stare. His copper-colored eyes were rimmed with thick lashes that would make a set of fake ones insecure. He lifted a hand to get the attention of a server and ordered me something girly to drink.

I picked at a napkin.

"I'll be honest, I wasn't sure that you would show up at all tonight."

So used to seeing him in a formal suit, it had never crossed my mind how sexy he would look in blue jeans a white button-down. Damn. It had been too long, and he was too good looking. So as not to gawk at his perfectly carved muscles underneath his shirt, I looked into his eyes again. They were locked onto my breasts. *Alright, still a pig. Got it.* I shifted uncomfortably in my seat and cleared my throat.

"Yeah, um, me neither. I've been pretty busy with dad and Ava."

"Well, I'm glad you did."

That makes one of us. I politely smiled at him but allowed myself a glance around the room. The only thing that grabbed my attention was a rather large man sitting at the far end of the bar. His entire body was turned in my direction, his face mostly concealed under a hood. Who the hell wears a hoodie into a bar? Weirdos. That's who.

"Here you are." The chipper waitress put a martini glass filled with dark red liquor in front of me and a Budweiser, tall-neck, in front of Ben. "Can I get you anything else?"

I shook my head in sync with Benjamin's, tapping my foot to the rhythm of the blaring rock music to prevent myself from leaping up and making up a poor excuse to head home. Would it really be so bad to just let myself have a night out? Maybe. I threw back my drink and let him order me another.

This cycle repeated a few times as the bar began to quickly fill with people, so much that our waitress couldn't keep up. Ben jumped at the opportunity to be chivalrous. I waited at the table while he went to buy us another round at the bar. When he returned, he seemed to contemplate my glass for a moment.

"Something wrong?" I asked.

"Got this one for free, compliments of that guy," He said, sliding it in my direction and nodding toward the bar. I followed his eyes to the weirdo who was still facing me.

I should have refused it, and everything inside of me screamed to do so. Instead, in my fuzzy state of mind, I took a long pull from the glass. Prickling heat oozed down my throat. My head started to spin immediately, causing me to stand, feeling the alcohol warm in my belly and heavy on my eyelids.

"Excuse me for a sec?"

Without waiting for a response, I headed for the sign marked 'women.' My eyes wandered briefly to the weirdo man at the bar. His legs shifted as if he was thinking about walking over to me. I quickly looked away, not wanting to open that can of worms.

The door swung open easier than I had anticipated and I stumbled forward. I nearly fell face-first onto the cheap tile, but my fingers managed to find purchase on the counter underneath the chipped mirror. The lights in the poorly lit restroom flickered as I pulled myself back to a standing position. My reflection wiggled and warped, making my stomach flip. I swallowed hard against the bile rising in my throat.

"Pull yourself together, it was only a few drinks," I told myself aloud. Somehow, I was the only one occupying the restroom. Where are all of the other women? You know, like in the movies, who go to hang out in bathrooms, when I need them? I slapped the faucet handle which resulted in a reluctant sputtering of just enough water to splash onto my face. With another glance at myself, I noticed my cheeks had grown hot and almost as red as my hair.

I didn't care that my carefully drawn eyeliner was streaming down my cheeks. The cold water was reviving some of my senses, but only slightly. My head was swimming, my palms slick with sweat. I made my way back into the bar. Weirdo was nowhere to be seen, and I decided not to find Ben and tell him goodbye. I had one thing on my mind; I was very drunk and needed to get home immediately.

I shoved my way through the factions of sweaty bodies. People were asking me if I was okay, the looks on their faces were probably that of worry. But asking for aid wasn't something I was willing to swallow my pride to do.

Outside, the sky had darkened to a rich, deep azure with

freckles of bright stars. The humid air hit my body. It weighed on my feet, causing them to drag with each step. *Damn heels. I never wear heels, why did I think this was a good idea?*

"You forgot something," snarled a deep voice from over my shoulder. I spun around as fast as my inebriated body would allow. Squinting, I could make out the shape of a handbag. It swayed against the breeze as it dangled from the fingers of a tall figure. Tall might be an understatement. This guy was enormous . . . and he was also the weirdo from the bar.

"Thanks." I slurred, snatching my purse from him. I turned to continue my journey home and worked at keeping my head low. I could hear his heavy boots marching in time to the click of my heels against the pavement. My heart began to thud wildly in my chest. Drawing my feet forward with as much force as I could muster, I quickened my pace. He did the same.

This was it. I couldn't believe I was about to be murdered by some creep I saw in a bar. It's what I get for going out once a year. My intuition advised that I run, and the rest of me did its best to obey. The only task I could perform was kicking off my cheap heels before taking off in a stumbling sprint.

I ran as hard as I could. Block number one whizzed by, and then the second. The alleyway I rounded into was one that leads to a street just a few houses down from mine. Footfalls were no longer thumping behind me. I continued straining to pick up even the faintest sound. Nothing.

I slowed to a halt and put my hands on my knees as I hunched forward, gasping for air. I could feel vomit rising in my throat and, without further warning, expelled the drinks I'd had all over the ground. Just as I had steadied myself enough to stop retching, gravel crunched to my left. Shooting up, I stumbled while backing away from the noise. My eyes flicked over the darkness, and I could feel my pulse pumping adrenaline through me from scalp to sole.

"Who's there?" I shouted.

I don't know why I asked, I didn't even want the answer. But I got it regardless. Weirdo emerged from the shadows. My heart stopped at the display of two gleaming spheres beneath the hood. They were ruby-red and glowing like there was a fire burning within them.

"What the h—"

The man rushed at me with inhuman speed. In seconds he held me pinned against the brick wall of a building. I kicked him and clawed at the arm he had pushed against my throat. My lungs tried desperately to fill with air. My eyes bulged, stinging with tears.

Digging my fingernails against his forearm was a worthless attempt against his hard-as-stone skin, and he didn't so much as flinch when I brought a foot into his groin. With ease, he shoved me further up the wall. My lungs were beginning to ache, my head filled with pressure.

With his free hand, the man dragged a heavy hand along my exposed thigh. I assumed the worst was about to happen. But instead, he seized my wrist, causing searing pain to tunnel up through my forearm and ascend into my shoulder. I wanted to scream, or call for help, but I didn't.

"I look forward to seeing your participation in the Trials, hag." He growled in a low, distorted tone. A putrid stench saturated my nostrils, making my stomach lurch.

My knees slammed into the rough earth as he released me, and my hand flew to my throat. Coughing stung my chest and rocked my body as I attempted to stop myself from gagging. From the corner of my eye, I could make out his outline.

"Wait!" I rasped just before he stepped inside the shadows.

He twisted on his heel, an amused smirk displaying over his lips. I lifted to my feet, gradually as to not tip forward and eat dirt.

"Who are you?" My nose was either runny from the puking, or it was dripping blood. I wasn't sure which. Wiping the wetness from my lips, I took a step toward the hooded freak. He waited, unmoving and patient.

"I am the creature that nightmares are made of, little Witch. You'd do well to remember that." He sneered through rows of sharp, yellowing teeth before stepping into the darkness. At this point, there was no doubt in my mind about this guy not being a human.

"Witch?" I repeated, but he had already gone. Tears drenched my face. The stinging in my throat was almost as bad as that in my arm. I decided it best to get the heck out of there. Grabbing my purse, I ran as fast as my feet could carry me. I wasn't satisfied until I had returned home and shoved my way through the door. After a triple-check that the lock and deadbolt were both clicked into place, my knees buckled. I slid down the door, resting against it as my shoulder shook with sobs, my face buried in my palms. My brain was still hazy from the drink, not even the adrenaline had burned it from my veins.

I sat there, crying like a lost child until the pain in my wrist had become nothing more than a dull throb. Pulling myself together as best I could, I rose and made my way to the bathroom. With the heat turned all the way up, I stepped into the shower. The blood on my hands confirmed that it had, in fact, been my nose bleeding. *Great.* My wrist burned but, upon examining it, I could see that there was nothing more than a slight red tint on the skin there. No indication of a needle or knife wound, though it felt like my arm had been injected with rattlesnake venom.

I let the water run cold before shutting the faucet off and making my way to bed. Clothing didn't even cross my mind. I just needed to sleep and forget anything had ever happened. Just before toppling onto the bed, my cell sounded off in the living room. *Ava.* I rushed to my bag. Pulling out my phone, I hit the green button and the words flew out before I could stop them.

"Ava? Are you okay? What happened?"

"Hey, um, everything is fine... you told me to call and check in, remember?" She sounded annoyed. I shut my eyes and sighed. Relief washed over me as my heart began to settle back into a reasonable pace.

"I remember, sorry. Things got a little weird tonight."

"Well, we just left the movie theater, heading to Ashley's now. I'll call you in the morning."

Ava disconnected before I could say anything else. Maybe I had startled her into thinking that I'd changed my mind about letting her stay out all night. I decided to leave it at that and settled for sending her a text that said: "I love you."

It was enough for me to know that nothing had happened to her. I went back to my bedroom and made sure the volume on my phone was all the way up before sliding under the covers. Despite my hopes of forgetting the strange encounter, my mind swam with questions. Why didn't he kill me, or worse? What did he mean by saying he looked forward to my participation? Participation in what exactly? He had also called me a Witch...

Chapter Three

Bzzz Bzzz Bzzz

I grunted and threw a hand around my phone. With a headache pounding against my temples, I looked at the screen and accepted the call.

"Hey, Ava."

"Are you still sleeping? It's, like, two in the afternoon Eden. Did you stay out all night with Mr. Tall, Dark and Handsome? You said things got weird, was it in a good way? Tell me everything!"

Two o'clock? Regardless, it was too early for this crap. I hadn't even had any caffeine yet. I blinked the sleep from my eyes and sat up with a yawn.

"No, just tired is all. How was your night?"

"It was great! I'm going to stay another night at Ashley's if you are cool with it. Her family is taking a trip down to the lakes today and I really want to go, pretty please?"

"Ava, I think you should come home today. I could use some help around the house. Plus, you promised you would find a summer job. Have you even started looking for one?"

I rubbed my eyes and climbed out of bed while waiting for her response. Sifting through my dresser drawers, I could hear her chatting with someone else for a minute.

"I promise I will, Eden. I just want to do this one thing. Please?"

"Fine." I sighed.

"Oh my god, thank you, Eden. You're the best."

"But call me later. Wear sunscreen. Don't go near that water without a life jacket."

"Yeah, sure."

"I'm serious."

"I said, okay. I love you, call you later."

The line went dead. I tossed the phone onto my mattress and removed some shorts and a tank top from the drawer. The shirt grazed my wrist as I pulled it on, sending a tingle up to my elbow. The recollection of the previous night overwhelmed my mind. I jerked my arm in front of my face to inspect the injury. But what I found wasn't a wound. In fact, I didn't know what the heck it was.

A star with seven points shone on the surface of my skin. It didn't penetrate my flesh, but instead sat atop it, like a glyph. My eyes were wide, my mouth hanging loose as I pulled a finger through it. The points curled at the touch, sending another odd tingle through my arm.

I hurried to the bathroom. With trembling fingers, I wet a washcloth and scrubbed at the peculiar mark until my skin had become raw. Nothing happened. I cursed and ran back to my room, thrusting open my laptop screen. After a quick search, numerous articles popped up for the distinct star. I clicked the first link.

"A Faerie star."

I compared my mark to the picture on the computer screen. They were identical. Still, if it had come from that creep, it hadn't been there last night. Right? Had I just ingested too much alcohol and dreamed the whole thing? Perhaps I had just become so inebriated that I had stumbled into an underground tattoo parlor using experimental ink.

"Yeah, that's more likely, Eden," I murmured to myself.

The doorbell echoed out in short chimes, causing me to jump in my skin. Seizing my cell phone, I walked down the hall and cautiously approached the front door. Able to see the silhouette of a man, I slowly unbarred the locks and cracked the door an inch. Peering outside, my shoulders sank in relief as I pulled the door further open.

"Hey, Ben." I did my best to greet him, squinting against the dazzling sunlight stabbing my eyes.

"Hey Eden, I uh..." He scratched his scalp. A frown was stretched tightly across his face.

"Come on in. I was just about to make some coffee."

He looked down, kicking at the step with his tennis shoe, he nodded in compliance. Moving aside so that he could enter, I motioned toward the kitchen and lead the way. He hunkered down at the oval table while I brewed a fresh pot of coffee for the pair of us.

"Eden, you don't have to do that," He started. Oh, but I did, I really did.

"I just wanted to stop by to make sure that you were alright. You kind of disappeared last night."

"Yeah," I answered, pouring us each a glassful and handing his off before settling down alongside him. "There was just something that came up. I'm sorry, truly."

I took a careful sip from my mug, permitting the caffeine to eat away at my pounding headache.

"I get that. I just wish you would have called me. I was worried about you."

I could see he was being honest. His warm, chocolate-eyes were gentle and full of concern. I sensed my bottom lip tremble, aching to tell him everything but knew it was probably best not to. He would deem me crazy. Forcing my lip to behave itself, I looked back at him and gave a meek half-smile.

"Thanks for caring, Benjamin. I just really needed to get back home in a rush. It was nothing against you..."

"Everything okay with Ava? Your dad?"

"Yeah, yeah...they are good."

We sat in silence for a while, the only sound emanated from my fingernails rapping the ceramic coffee cup clutched tightly between my palms. Out of nowhere, Ben's hand encircled my wrist. I recoiled, remembering abruptly what was on it. What if he noticed?

"I think you should go."

Ben's brows pulled together, and he drew his hand back in a hurry.

"Sorry. I just don't know what you're expecting of me right now."

"I didn't mean anything by it, Eden. I just wanted you to know that I'm here for you if you need someone to talk to."

Go figure. Mister ego had a personality outside of being a tool. He pushed his chair back and stood to head out. I pinched the bridge of my nose before setting my cup down and following him to the door.

"Ben?"

He turned.

"Thanks...for the date, but also for checking up on me."

That abnormally white smile spread across his face. He gave me a wink that nearly melted me to a puddle before pulling the door open and taking a step halfway out. He turned back.

"Let me know when you are ready for a second?"

I smiled back at him and nodded.

"I will, I promise."

He closed the door, and I was left to my empty house and thoughts again. Not knowing what to make of everything that happened, I retreated to the table. Coffee served me well for the better half of the day. I sat there, gulping down the entire pot, plus the cup Ben had neglected to drink. Tidying the house here and there, my headache dwindled and ultimately became nothing more than an annoyance at the back of my skull.

By dinner time, my belly was gurgling in protest to my dismissing the need to feed it for a full day. Our freezer was usually packed full of frozen goodness, so I grabbed a random box and pushed it into the microwave. Salisbury steak in gravy with mashed potatoes and corn. It wasn't my first choice in a meal, but it would be enough to pacify my stomach.

With one hand full of piping hot food, the other holding a tall glass of black tea, I headed to the couch. Flipping through television shows, I polished off the bland meal. It was a distraction. What I craved was to think about what had transpired the night before. To analyze every second of it. To figure out what the hell that freak was talking about when he called me a "little Witch."

My cell phone hummed with a text.

"Thinking about you." I smiled at the message from Ben.

Holding the phone with clammy fingers, I thought of a reply. I could give him a shot, like, a real shot. It wouldn't kill me to have a steady relationship with someone outside of my family. It might even be enjoyable. Who knew how long it had been since I had had a partner in my bed? It was definitely before I became a mother figure to Ava rather than an older sister. I suppose that I felt accountable for her, to the point that I didn't even want to try at a connection with anyone else. I wanted to focus on her, make sure her path was paved.

Still, I'm human, and I have needs too...I picked up the phone and tapped the screen. Pulling up the text message, I wrote back and pushed send. The reply from Ben was virtually instantaneous.

"Next weekend sounds great!!"

A rap on the door made me jump. I hurried to pitch my dinner trash away and smoothed my hair before strolling to the door to pull it open. An empty porch awaited me. I moved into the cooling, dark air.

"Hello?"

I turned back to look at my cell phone, sitting on the couch several feet indoors. I had to be imagining things. Probably too much coffee. I shuffled back inside and shut the door. Once settled on the couch again, I checked my phone. No new messages. My shoulders slumped in disappointment. Oh well, it was getting late, and sleep didn't sound like too bad of an idea.

Just as I started preparing myself to get up, something clattered to the floor down the hall, forcing me to me spring to my feet much quicker than I had planned to. With a glance at the door, I pondered whether to just run through it. I persuaded myself not to, thinking that I needed to stop being a baby, and tiptoed forward. Making my way down the hall, I peered into Ava's room as I passed. Nothing in there.

My bedroom sat at the end of the hall, I observed that my door still was how I had left it, wide open. The floorboards creaked from somewhere behind me, which caused my feet to freeze in place. Had that come from the living room? Slowly, I turned my head. A figure stood, staring at me from down the hall. My chest tightened, a scream forming in my throat.

"If you are thinking of screaming for help, think twice. I will close that mouth myself before you can so much as whimper."

It was that distorted voice again, the one belonging to the man from the night before. Every ounce of my being cried at me to run, to get out of there and never look back. My chest heaved as I turned the rest of my body to face the invader. The outcry reabsorbed into my lungs.

"What do you want?" I asked with an unsteady voice, taking a step backward toward my room. There had to be something in there I could use to defend myself. Fear stirred inside of me as he stepped closer.

"Stay back!" I thrust a hand out. He hesitated before taking another step. Chills coursed through me. I worked to take deep gulps air as my hands fell upon the door frame to my room.

"You are late to answer your call to the duty of your Coven. I'm a bounty hunter. I've come to collect you."

"What are you talking about, you freak?" My throat was growing tight. The fear in me was building, morphing into something more. I figured a panic attack was on the way. With his next step, the fright began to feel like pure energy, I could feel it burning a hole inside of me.

"My name is not 'freak.'"

Gleaming red eyes probed me. There was still a hood atop his head, but it was different from before. Judging by his mostly shapeless form, I figured that he was wearing a cloak. I twisted my face in every direction looking for something, anything, to use against him. The floorboards groaned in protest to his weight as he moved closer still. Hot breath poured down my back.

The thing inside of me split wide open at that moment. Whatever it was, it had hit its peak. White-hot energy crawled over my skin. I looked down with wide eyes to find that *actual* energy flashes were traveling between my fingers. The little electricity bolts coiled around my knuckles and began to strike up my forearms. It was like watching a lightning storm. A hiss sounded behind my ear.

I did the only thing I could think of, which was to twirl around and plant a fist straight into the intruder's snout. The current surged outward once the contact was established. It raced from my fingers and branched out across his face, which was pinched in anticipation. I observed in horror as he tore at the bolts, trying to pull the web of electricity apart. I jerked back as it fizzled out, leaving his face smoking. With a clenched jaw, he lunged at me.

"Think you can beat me, little witch?" he roared, clutching my throat, and hoisting me three feet above the floor. His grip contracted just enough to cut the oxygen from entering my airways. Efforts to pull myself loose weren't working, so I changed tactics. Self-defense videos I occasionally partook in say to 'go for the eyes,' so that's what I did in my frantic state of mind.

His face was still smoldering from the energy blast I had somehow just conjured. I could feel the burning strands as I struck his face. Putting what little knowledge I had into action, I pushed the hood back, fully intent on doing what must be done. With eyebrows drawn tightly together, I watched the hood tumble across his shoulders and down his back. His obsidian skin was riddled with designs. The fervent ruby eyes bore into my soul, his anger feeding through me, all the way to the tip of my toes.

But my eyes weren't secured on his, they were studying the twisted black horns growing from each side of his skull. There were two, bending wickedly around the crown of his head. Holy Hell. Wriggling and thrashing, I urgently tried to get away from the monster attacking me. His grip slackened enough for me to take in a deep breath before he released me to the floor.

Chapter Four

"You use that filthy Witch power on me again, and I will kill you. King's gold be damned, I won't let my status be sullied by Witch markings."

"What are you?" I cried with more terror in my voice than I thought was possible. A laugh thundered from his chest in a way that made my skin crawl. He replaced the hood, taking care to pull it low onto the bridge of his nose.

"Even with a crushed throat, she speaks."

He thrust the same hand that had just been wrapped around my throat into my face. I didn't accept it and instead gawked at him as I rose to my feet on my own. He dropped his fist and proceeded to watch me struggle to get up.

"Can you at least tell me what it is that you want from me? Without blocking my windpipe, preferably?"

"As I told you before, you are due elsewhere."

"What does that even mean? What are you?"

"The name of my kind is Demon. Just as you are a Witch."

He said the word like it left a bad taste on his tongue.

"Yeah, got that much," I steadied myself. I was really in no position to get snappy with this thing, Demon, whatever. Maybe the fact that I had already expected him to kill me, twice, with no results was leaving me a bit cocky. Not that I was complaining about him not killing me, yet. "What is it that I am supposed to be doing?"

"You should have answered the call to your birthplace by now, to compete in the Fae Prince's little games. Your mother's Coven expects your participation."

"My...mother? How do you know my mother?"

Either this guy was playing some kind of sick joke, or he wanted me to do that little magic trick again.

"I don't have time for chatting. If you want to know more, you can find someone to converse within Blaive's castle."

"You came here to do what? Take me to a castle? I think I deserve some kind of answers!" He closed the distance between us. The same foul odor from the night before surrounded me.

"Listen and listen well. Time goes by quickly while I'm here. So quickly, in fact, that it has taken a week of my time to find you. If I don't get you to Blaive soon, my payment will become forfeit. Do you know what that means for you, pretty little Witch?" He toyed with a curl on my shoulder, sending a shiver down my spine.

"It means that you will have cost me a job that could feed me for a year. If you are of no use to me," He released the lock and came in even closer. "I will discard you and let your prince find the pieces I leave behind."

"And if I refuse the prince?" I stood as tall as I could manage.

Only then, I heard Ava's singsong voice calling for me through the house.

"Eden? Where are you?"

The Demon spared a glance over his shoulder and looked back at me with that wicked grin, showing every pointed tooth in his disgusting mouth.

"Then the next in line to your mother's throne will take your place. Make your decision."

He erupted into spirals of black vapor, disappearing from the room. Ava's footfalls hammered down the hallway. She reached the doorway and flipped the light on, staring at me with a scowl.

"Why are you standing alone in the dark? And what the heck is that smell? Are you smoking in here?"

I gazed back at her, my heart descending in my chest. He had meant her. If I withdrew, Ava would be required to go in my place. What if both of us refused? I trembled at the thought while she made her way over to me.

"Are you alright, Eden? It looks like you've seen a ghost or something."

I threw my arms around her and did my best to keep the tears stinging my eyes at bay.

"Eden, what is going on?"

Ava leaned back so she could look into my eyes. The scowl intensified.

"Um, nothing," I sniffed and released her.

"It's just, I need to go...I got a job offer. The interview is in New York City. I fly out tonight."

"What? Eden, I came home to tell you that the hospital has been trying to get ahold of you. Dad isn't doing so hot. You can't just leave now."

My throat constricted. A sob threatened to escape from deep in my breast. Wanting to throw my arms around her again and explain it all, I knew I couldn't. Not only would she not believe me, but I might be putting her life in danger if I did.

"I'm sorry Ava," I choked. "It's just something I have to do. Dad is strong, he will pull through like he always does. Please, can you just let him know that I'm thinking of him?"

Ava glowered at me in disbelief. Taking a step away from me, she looked as though I had just slapped her in the face. In a way I had. Dad meant the world to both of us. He wasn't doing so hot already, which meant a call from the hospital could suggest he would be gone soon. But I didn't have a choice. I had to protect Ava, at any cost. I had promised to do so.

"You're unbelievable Eden. Have fun on your trip while Dad is dying in a hospital bed."

She spun around and stormed out of the room and down the hall. A tear fell from my cheek as I heard the door slam behind her. The words felt like a red-hot poker in my heart. Standing in my bedroom, I took a quick glance around before tossing as many of my possessions as I could fit inside a duffle bag. I collected everything I thought that I might need.

Clothes, a toothbrush, some hair ties. I didn't know what to expect, nor what would be beneficial to me wherever we were traveling to. Murky vapor permeated the room as the Demon reappeared. I didn't turn to confront him while he watched in stillness as I threw as much of my life as I could carry into the bag.

"Harper."

His voice startled me. I paused in between zipping up the bag and slinging it over my shoulder.

"What?"

"My name, it's Harper."

"Sounds oddly human," I replied flatly.

Harper half snorted, half chuckled at the remark. I was pretty sure I had just insulted him, not that I cared in the slightest. Strolling into the living room, I set down the bag to slide on a weathered pair of sneakers that were long overdue for a replacement.

"So," I straightened and reached for the duffle bag. "Where are we headed?"

Harper seized my belongings before I could, and much more easily lifted it and motioned toward the door. So now he chooses to act polite. Thirty minutes ago he was longing to exterminate me.

"The forest."

Odd place to be going. I was partially convinced he was pointing me to a place of isolation just so he would have a nice spot to butcher me in. Not having much of a choice in the affair, I started forward, leading us out of the door and up the street. Despite the late hour, I prayed someone would be awake to see us and call the police. Not that it would do any good, this guy was seven feet worth of sheer, lethal power.

The forest line wasn't far outside of city limits. The trees towered overhead, watching menacingly as I took the first steps inside. I felt a profound sense of grief. Understanding from that moment on, my life was about to take a turn. For better or worse, I was wholly immersed now.

"I don't exactly have a map, Harper. Would you mind taking the lead now?"

Disregarding me, he proceeded to follow as I wandered through the brush. Everything about the forest creeped me out at night. Critters didn't scamper within the greenery and the air was too still. It produced an eerie calm, nothing to be heard save for the sound of twigs snapping under my sneakers. We trekked for what seemed like hours before he decisively advanced, pushing a forearm against my chest.

"This will do."

He reached into the cloak at his throat, drawing out a silver chain. At the end of it dangled a gem, amber in shade, it shimmered despite the darkness. Harper took a few steps ahead and set his heavy boots securely into the ground. Chanting something unintelligible under his breath, he pulled the jewel through the air, holding it like he was an artist, and it was his paintbrush. In the wake of it, glimmering radiance displayed in words that were foreign to me. He worked at it until an enormous symbol glistened in front of him.

"*Brruntek*."

At his command, the glyph divided, bleeding with a blinding glare. I thrust up a hand to shield my eyes that had adjusted to the dark.

"Come," Harper ordered, elbowing me toward it.

"I'm not going anywhere near that thing, are you insane?"

He gave my shoulder a shove with a massive hand. Groaning, I knew that whether I wanted to or not, I was about to descend into this magical freaking hole. I peered at him over my shoulder, confident that my face was saturated with dread. He pointed to the core, where the opening was glittering, hungry and waiting for me.

"Inside. Now." He commanded.

"You don't have to be so bossy," I muttered and stretched out a hand to test its solidity. It felt strange, like my fingers were inside of a gooey vacuum. Despite the strangeness of it all, the gateway lured me with warmth. My chest tightened. What if he had the wrong girl? What if the mysterious opening could sense that, and was about to melt my face off? What if...

With another firm shove from Harper, the decision was made for me. Entering it felt like the times I had dreamt of slipping from a cliff's edge. It was the kind of dream that jolted you awake in the middle of the night. Only, I couldn't rouse as I proceeded to descend down into the magical rabbit hole. My limbs slung outward, urgently seeking something to take hold of, to steady the spinning. My eyes had forced themselves closed against the light. An ungodly amount of time passed while I tumbled down until I finally slammed into the hearty terrain.

The spinning ceased just as abruptly as it had begun. I groaned and pushed myself up with unsteady arms. Leaning back on my heels, I cracked my eyes to examine the area, expecting the hell itself. Seeing only the forest floor, I elevated my gaze. We were right where we had started. Harper landed on his feet beside me and I was pretty sure the whole forest shuddered.

"It didn't work."

"Look again," He grunted and hauled me to my feet without warning.

My eyes scanned the woods while I accompanied him in trudging onward. The forest was the same...and different.

Lustrous emerald and azure fungi spread from the base all the way up into the canopy of the dark trees. In spite of the nighttime, everything appeared so vivid and full of life.

"What is this place?" I asked in awe.

"This," He answered, kicking a spiraling iridescent plant out of his way. "Is the Faewild, it encompasses the castle. Be grateful you have me with you. Conditions can get rather dicey for novice Fae-kind roaming through here."

Considering every word emanating from his chops, I hastened my aching feet to settle into stride alongside him.

"How far is it, the castle?"

"Not far."

"And how far is not far?"

"Keep quiet."

Chewing my cheek while we walked, I accepted his request, keeping silent along the trail of wild luminescent plants and flora, only looking up once we had entered the clearing. Glad to be past the clusters of trees, impressive as they were, I required unrestricted air. Beyond us was unlike anything I had encountered before. I observed the hues of color above as they weaved in and out of each other lazily, their backdrop a splattering of twinkling stars and dark azure sky.

Beneath the display, I could make out the colossal outline of a stone wall. Behind the wall was what I could only assume to be the castle spires. My heart trembled at the idea that I was moments away from unearthing what exactly was transpiring here. Suddenly I felt very nauseous. What if I didn't want to know?

Two guards stood at attention against the wall, a barrier elevated behind them. Silver armor flashed beneath rows of golden leaves, giving them the appearance of scale mail. Their fists chimed as they traveled to the hilt of their weapons at the sight of Harper and me. I halted in place, while Harper elevated his hands to display that we had arrived free of weapons.

"Hold there, Demon."

"Easy fellows, I've come to deliver this hag to Lord Blaive."

With that, he nudged me forward, ignoring my pinched face at his remark. The guard to the left studied my appearance for a moment and jerked his fingers at the other, a signal to disengage the gate.

"We will take her to Blaive from here. You're free to leave, Demon."

"What about my payment?" Harper roared, making even the fully suited guard quake in his boots.

"You should know the laws by now. Come back at dawn to speak with Lord Blaive. He will honor the transaction and have the gold transported to you."

Harper scowled at me, presumably wishing he hadn't chosen to bring me the entire way in one night. To be honest, I was pretty glad that I didn't have to worry about it. A third guard reported after the gate had been dropped.

"Take the Witch to her quarters, I'll send word to Lord Blaive." The first guard said to number three. "If she so much as twitches her fingers, don't hesitate to do what you must for your prince."

"What the hell does that mean?" I argued.

All of them disregarded my question, the third firmly taking hold of my forearm. I looked over at Harper who stood in place, as though he were prepared to argue for the rest of eternity, so long as he got his money. I wasn't his problem anymore. He continued cursing at the gatekeeper until we were well out of earshot. A feeling of overwhelming loneliness hit me right in the gut. He may have protected me in the forest but he wasn't about to do more than what he was making money for.

Holding my arm much harder than I deemed necessary, the guard escorted me into a darkened and quiet city. In the dim light, I was only capable of catching glimpses of intricately constructed buildings. The castle became clearer the further in we walked. It towered overhead, with torches blazing all around it. Amethyst flames lit the heavy three-story doors at the entrance. More guards were posted there, and I was sure hundreds more were dispersed throughout the place. They opened the doors for us to pass through.

"Why are the flames purple?"

"In celebration of The Trials. Now shut your mouth."

The innards of the castle were also dimly illuminated in the late hours. Torches flickered, casting shadows across the hall. It gave me the creeps, leaving me to feel like I was strolling into a dungeon. The only sound was the clanking of metal from the guard's armor as he led us down numerous hallways. Hundreds of doors later, I was completely lost.

Finally, we settled outside of a door that jutted slightly ajar.

"You're quarters, hag." His voice was deep and came out like rumbling thunder clouds.

I peered at his odd yellow eyes, awaiting further instructions. It quickly became apparent that he had nothing else to say to me. I pulled free of his grasp to face the door. It was elegantly crafted from dense timber, with golden vines twisting and looping through each other to form a Celtic knot. Setting a palm upon it, I used every ounce of strength that was left in me to push against it.

Groaning in a pleasant, low rumble, the door swung open, revealing a large room. The tall ceiling overhead was covered in artwork. Drapes of rich burgundy hung from the windows. I stepped further in, inhaling the smoky aroma wafting from the crackling hearth. A queen-sized bed rested opposite of the glowing fireplace with a canopy erected above it. Elegant, sheer fabric hung from it in soft folds that tumbled to the floor.

An assortment of chests and other containers were arranged around the room. Crap. Harper had my freaking clothes.

"Excuse me," I spun around to find that the guard had already gone.

"Great. So much for my things I guess."

"You don't need them." Spoke a low, strong voice from across the chamber.

"Excuse me?" I slowly shuffled around the bed, my heart hammering against my breast. An ivory table rested on the other side. Two chairs were beside it, one of them being occupied. I grimaced at what I could only presume was the back of a cloaked man. What was with these people and their stupid cloaks? The man rose casually. Twisting to face me, he drew back the hood.

I'm rather certain that my heart stopped beating the moment I laid eyes on him. With his perfectly carved jaw, eyes as pale and green as seafoam, and skin a robust espresso color, he was absolute perfection. He swung a hand toward the door, which clicked shut in obedience. Removing the cloak from his broad shoulders, he tossed it onto the bed and ran a thumb across his smooth, square jaw. I observed him doing so in complete and utter reverence. He wasn't as tall as Harper had been, but close enough. His muscular build was apparent, even underneath the elegant attire that clung to him.

"I'm Rowan." He said simply.

"Eden Morris," I responded, pushing a hand toward him in greeting. Before I realized what was happening, he seized my hand and had me twirled around, bending it up behind my back in a matter of seconds. His body heat raced over me in waves that smelled of spiced wine and the Faewild. I could feel his breath on the exposed skin at my nape. With his groin pushed securely against my backside, I was having a difficult time figuring out what he was doing.

"Careful with swift movements here, Witch."

There was that word again.

"I'm getting really tired of you people calling me that. I have a name, as I just told you."

"I know who you are."

"Oh yeah? And how is that exactly?"

"It's my duty, as future Fae King, to know everything about the other nobles in the Realm. We didn't think you would make an appearance. *And*," He growled in my ear. His voice was gruff, sending a shiver up my spine.

"You're late."

Chapter Five

"WHAT ARE YOU TALKING ABOUT? YOUR DEMON STOPPED BY last night and then again tonight. I wasn't exactly given a memo." Wriggling against his hold, I tried to free myself, quickly realizing that it was impossible.

"Watch how you speak to me, wit--"

"Don't even say it. My name is Eden. Can you please let go of me now?"

He twisted my arm further up, causing my back to arch. My head fell against his collarbone with a thud that jarred my teeth. He must have been leaning down because there was no way I should have been able to do that. His breathing remained steady in my ear, calm, collected. Everything I was not at that moment.

"I am not part of your nasty little Coven, I am the prince of this kingdom, and you will address me as such when you open that vile, Witch mouth of yours."

"I'm sorry," I winced at the ache he was creating in my shoulder. "But you asked me here. I'm a guest by force, not choice. And I still don't even know what the hell I'm here to do. Prince Rowan." I added the last bit for good measure.

"You are here because it is required of you. I didn't write the law that brought you, but I will enforce it. Even if it means allowing a Witch into my home."

"Can you please let go of my arm? I don't even understand how I zapped Harper, so I'm fairly positive I won't be doing it again."

Rowan slackened his hold of me, enabling me to break free and put a foot or two of distance between us. I stroked my wrist and grimaced at his stupid, handsome face. His loose black curls dangled in a perfect border around his jawline. I could also see the tip of a pointed ear beneath the mass of impressive hair.

"You can't activate your spells? Why?" His voice was firm and demanding. I eyed him despite my bowed head.

"I don't have spells, I don't have a Coven, I don't know where I am or why I'm here."

"You said you did something before, though, to the Demon I hired. Who is a week late, might I add, and won't be getting paid."

"I bet he will be jumping for joy at the news." I sighed and rubbed my arm, which was still stinging from his grip. I shook the thought of Harper's threat to kill me if Rowan didn't pay up from my mind and tried to focus on what we had been talking about.

"When Harper came to collect me, I accidentally made some lightning stuff attack his face. I don't know how I did it. One second I was frightened; the next, my fists were covered with the stuff."

"I don't believe you." He sneered, his eyes never leaving mine. I felt small under his gaze, especially because he was impeccable and stood a full foot and a half taller than me. Seriously, it was like an artist had created him with the tears of an angel. Perfect, in every way.

"Believe me, don't believe me. I don't care. Just tell me what I have to do to get back home. Please."

He considered me for a minute. I stood there like I was being lectured, feeling naked under his pale eyes as they scanned me up and down. Eventually, he sat back down and pointed at the other chair with a long finger.

"Sit."

I obliged, far too exhausted to get myself man-handled again. Once my bottom hit the chair I was pretty confident that I could fall asleep, right then and there. Instead, I held his stare with my own and waited for him to start talking.

"You are here to participate in the Devotion Trials. In these Trials, that will occur over the next week, you will be challenged by six others."

He reached a hand across the table, palm up and wiggled his impeccable fingers at me. I grudgingly place my hand on his. He flipped it over to reveal the Faerie Star. Tracing it delicately enough to send ripples of desire through me, he explained how it worked.

"Each point represents a participant. When one is defeated, a point will brand into your skin. The one who finishes the Trial with all seven points will be the winner."

"What's the prize? I asked cautiously.

"My hand in marriage."

"Marriage?" I jumped to my feet, my mind spinning. Marriage would mean being trapped here forever.

"Yes, do you know what that is?"

"Of course I know what that is," I snapped with my head turned toward the door. I wanted nothing more than to run through it. I'd take my chances in the forest if it meant I didn't have to marry some arrogant jerk. Prince or not, this guy was way too full of himself for me to even consider it.

"But I don't want that, I don't even know you."

"I am in the midst of a century-long war, Witch. There are a dozen things I could be using this time for. Yet, I am sitting in a room that I am obligated to provide for a Witch, in the middle of the night."

His eyes grew dark and I could have sworn they shimmered

like stars falling from the sky. Suddenly the room went from warm and inviting, to cold and foreign. The longer I was around these creatures, the more it became apparent that they had a distaste for what they thought I was. Rowan moved closer, bringing his eyes level with my own. Despite feeling so small next to him, I stood my ground.

"I don't want you here any more than you want it. I'd love nothing more than to stop the silly Trials and send the lot of you away. Unfortunately, the law dictates that I cannot. Take comfort in knowing you are a weak, powerless little Witch. You won't make it past the first Trial."

Ouch, that was rough.

"What is your problem with Witches?" And why was I defending them? I wasn't one hundred percent sure that they had the right girl, despite the incident with Harper. Rowan squared his shoulders, returning to his full height, he thought about my words.

"My problem with Witches is that you and your kind are unpredictable. When I see a Demon, I know their evil intentions. Just as when I meet a Nymph, I know that they have nothing but good inside of them. Witches live in the grey area between light and dark. Your mother tipped that scale in the eyes of the king-dom, however."

Here we go again, someone I'd never met knew more than I did about my own mother.

"How did she do that?" I asked in a hushed tone. Rowan hesi-tated, his eyes locking with mine before he looked away.

"It matters naught, your mother has passed. That leaves you to take her place as Queen of the Coven. In turn, you are the most eligible of your kind to compete."

"What happens if I fail?" I swallowed hard against the dry ache in my throat.

"Should you fail or be bested, you will lose your status of nobility. But you will be free to return home."

"Sounds like a win-win."

He smiled, exposing a flash of perfect teeth. My heart fluttered, much to my disdain.

"Indeed. There is only one who I will support through the Trials, and that one is not you."

Rowan slapped a heavy palm upon the table and scooted back in his chair to stand. Not knowing the customary etiquette for being in the presence of a king-to-be, I followed his lead and stood to face him. That stare held a peculiar look as he eyed me without a word. It made me want to fling myself onto the bed and hide under the covers. I watched as the corner of his round bottom lip pulled upward.

"What?" I asked, digging fingernails into my palm.

"Nothing," He smirked and proceeded to move around me. As he did so, his knuckles brushed my bare thigh. The unintentional touch sent a layer of goosebumps darting across my skin. Had I not wanted to lightning punch that perfect nose and run for the hills, I might have savored it. But, of course, I did want to run, and he was the one forcing me to stay. The green eyes moved to mine, which had fallen to his lips for only a second. Much to my dismay, it caused him to pause mid-step.

"You are a lot less offensive on the eyes than most of your kind. I didn't expect that. Not that it is unheard of. Tamora wasn't a hag either."

Wow. Did he just call me 'not ugly'? And in the form of a compliment to my estranged mother.

"Well, thank you, but I don't think it matters what I look like. I'll be out of here after the first Trial."

"Please, see that you are."

Rowan walked to the large wooden armoire resting in the far corner and opened the twin doors to pull out clothing that shone like dewdrops on a spider's web. He cast it onto the bed and strolled through the door without missing a beat, his demeanor very much one that said he was someone in control.

The moment he had left and I heard the door click shut, I was at the window. My fingers were unsteady as I pulled up as hard as I could in an attempt to get at least one open wide enough to fit my slender body through. Repeating this method with each of them, I soon found out that they were stuck tight and I was left precisely where I had begun. With a speedy search of the room, I had a candlestick in hand and drawn over my shoulder, aiming straight at the polished glass.

Just before the sturdy metal could fly from my fingertips, something tugged at the back of my mind. If I did this, if I tried to escape, they would come for Ava. That is, if I could even find my way back to the woods, let alone the portal. My shoulders sank as I let the hoisted arm drop back to my side. Frustrated at the feeling of my life being so utterly out of my control, hot tears stung my eyes. I didn't want to let them fall. If I did, I wasn't sure they would ever stop.

Returning the candlestick to the bedside table, I shuffled across the lush carpet until I reached the skillfully folded garment Rowan had thrown at the bed. With a look down, I expelled a puff of air. As much as I didn't want to accept the gesture, my clothes looked like they had been dragged through a hog pen.

I removed the soiled shorts and tank top and pulled the beautiful silk gown over my head. It stretched just past my toes and felt like butter against my skin. Fine lace hung from the low neckline in a way that would have made a seamstress weep. My fingers traced the pattern as I scanned the space for a mirror. A vanity sat near the entrance. I approached to find a bowl of cool water with a clean white cloth draped over the side.

It wasn't a shower, but nevertheless, it felt great to wash as much of the grime from myself as I could. I took note of the bruises on my throat. A consequence of my two encounters with Harper, no doubt. I exhaled a sigh of satisfaction and eyed my reflection. Despite hours in a forest, and getting tossed around like a rag doll, my hair was still moderately tame. Studying the beautiful nightgown, I found that it hugged me in all the right spots. Under any other circumstances, I might have even whirled in it.

Rather than making a bigger fool of myself than I already had that day, I returned to the bed. It looked like paradise with the dense maroon quilt and down-stuffed pillows. I all too eagerly slithered into it. My body sank into what felt like a cloud. A remarkably warm, amazing cloud. Ava would have loved it.

Damnit. I brought my hands up my face and into my hairline. My cellphone had been in the duffle bag. Would there even be service to call home from another realm? No, presumably not. I'd just have to suffer in solitude without an occasional call to check up on my sister and father. Had I any option other than sacrificing my sister's well-being, I'd be out of here in a heartbeat.

Even if it meant wandering alone in a deadly Fae forest, I would have leaped at the opportunity. I stubbornly reminded myself that it was a waste of time to speculate. All I needed to do was wait for the ridiculous Trials to start. Then I'd allow myself to lose and be home in a flash. Even the prince himself didn't want me here. I guess him not being king yet meant he couldn't bend the laws at will. What is the point in being the leader of your own kingdom if you have no power over what occurs within it?

I shoved the image of the magical jerks from my mind. Trying to focus on what was important, I reminded myself of Ava. How she was always more interested in my social life than I was. How that was her way of showing her affection for me. And it worked, I never doubted my little sister's love for me, not once. Bickering with her about it was just a method of self-preservation.

I was lonely and Ava could see that, despite my constant effort to prove otherwise. She definitely would have been salivating over the stupid prince. Too bad he was the reason for me being in this mess to begin with, or I might be drooling too. Not that how I viewed him was relevant. If the rest of the competitors looked anything like him, I would be a weed amongst roses. I wasn't ugly by society's standards, I just wasn't a flawless elf, or whatever Rowan was.

Besides, he had already made it perfectly clear what he desired. It was the same thing that I did. For me to leave and forget I had ever been there.

Sleep weighed heavy on my eyelids the longer I mulled it over. No matter how much I didn't want to find out what the next day held in store for me, I couldn't fight slumber forever. Letting my eyes close, I relaxed my limbs and allowed dreams to take hold of my mind.

Chapter Six

"Miss? Miss?"

The unfamiliar voice startled me, rousing me from sleep. Ungluing my eyelids from each other, I gazed at the tiny, strange woman standing at the bedside. Clearing the sleep from my eyes, I sat up and elevated an eyebrow at her. She stood three feet high and had large ears that drooped over her small shoulders. Her shining golden eyes were wide, as her little fists hooked together at her bosom. She bobbed her head at me.

"Morning, miss, my name is Ellie. It is my pleasure to tell you that I will be your servant during the Trials. I didn't want to wake you, it's just that you've been sleeping most of the day and Prince Blaive is holding a reception in the grand hall. We've not got long to get you fed and outfitted."

The aroma of sausage and eggs permeated my nostrils. I launched the cover away and hopped down from the bed with a yawn at my lips. Holding a hand out at the woman, she looked startled and took a stride backward. Rolling my eyes, I lowered the hand and scratched my scalp with the other.

"Sorry, Ellie. I kind of forgot that I'm not supposed to do that. I'm Eden Morris."

"Not a problem mistress," Ellie offered a meek smile with giant eyes flicking between my hands and face, she gestured toward the spread on the table.

"I wasn't told what you prefer to eat, so I brought you a variety. I do hope it is to your liking. If not, I, of course, can return to the kitchens and have them make anything else you'd prefer."

My eyes darted over the platters of food, affirming that my nose had not deceived me. There was a white oval dish holding a mass of sausages. Another was filled with boiled eggs and perfectly baked bread. Jams, butter, spices, and an assortment of other things that I didn't recognize sat there, luring me. My belly gurgled in response.

"Thank you, Ellie," I said with a grin and took a seat to dig in.

"This will be perfect. It smells wonderful."

I sampled a taste of the spiced meat. Flavor erupted over my taste buds. I devoured at least four of them before slowing down enough to find Ellie beaming at me from across the table. Geez, where are my manners?

"I'm sorry. Would you like some?" I pushed the plate of sausages in her direction and began to slather jam onto the sweet-smelling bread. Ellie gave me a kind smile but shifted the plate aside.

"Many thanks, but I already had my breakfast as well as midday meal, mistress."

I nodded in response and resumed my feast until my stomach couldn't hold anymore. Ellie picked up on this and bustled over to the armoire, where she began to extract strikingly exquisite gowns of all different designs. She carefully arranged them in a spread across the edge of my bed.

"These aren't all the dresses we have for you, but they will be suitable for the occasion. I am also well-trained in facial art, as well as hair styling if you'd like, miss."

Not wanting to soil the fine garments, I cleaned my hands and face with the towel from the table before joining Ellie in examining the dresses. They were all so captivating, but I decided on a reasonably simplistic design. It was a long gown in my choice color, black. Radiant jewels were embroidered over the sweetheart bust in clusters that diminished as they went further down, creating a dazzling starburst of sparkle.

The flowy skirt hit exactly at the correct length, making it so it was long enough to touch the floor but not so long that it would trip me while I walked. Ellie helped me into it and laced up the corset rear, pulling it so that my breasts pushed up in just the right way. She moved back to examine me and nodded in approval.

"Great choice, miss. Now, onto the rest. We haven't much time now."

I let her work on my hair and face until she ultimately gasped in satisfaction, retreating to allow me a look at myself in the mirror. She had kept my face mostly natural, with a swipe of rich scarlet across my lips and a bit of shimmery eyeshadow beneath my full, arched eyebrows. Braids started at both of my temples and joined behind the crown of my head, sitting atop the long crimson curls that came to my waistline.

Just as Ava had a mere two days ago, Ellie left two locks down to frame my face.

"It looks lovely Ellie, thank you so much."

She attempted to suppress a wide grin and bowed again.

"Mister Ommin awaits just outside of the room. Shall I beckon him?"

"I'm sorry, who?"

"He will be your escort to the event, mistress."

"Ah, of course, let him inside, please." *Might as well act like I know what I'm doing here.*

"Enjoy your day, miss." She bowed a third time and retreated through the door. Before it could shut completely, a pale hand grasped it. In stepped a man with skin similar to the color of the moon. His straight black hair was tucked behind his ears and tied in a ponytail that hung past his wide shoulders. His piercing, azure eyes grew as they met mine.

"Wow..." The wide, full lips setting above his muscular jaw fell open in a gasp as he pulled me in for a hug. I grudgingly allowed his embrace and wondered if all the men here were going to be gorgeous because I really didn't think my libido could take that. He smelled wonderfully of herbs and embers. Once adequately satisfied with his first impression, he moved back with his hands still planted on my shoulders.

"Lady Eden, you look absolutely stunning. One might confuse you with Fae-kind."

"Just Eden, please." I said, "Thank you, mister...Ommin?"

"How silly of me," He patted a palm against his forehead and loosened his grip on me. "Yes, I'm Scott. I am your royal advisor, well, one of them. I will be guiding you through the Trials in the only way that I can; attempting to teach you to harness your abilities in the small amount of time that we have."

"Great. Except, I'll be losing, so it isn't necessary."

Scott withdrew, a strongly drawn frown taut over his lips.

"Why would you decide that you are going to fail?"

"Umm...I have no urge to marry a prince or perform in his contests. My father is dying, and my little sister is alone."

"Whoa," He huffed and returned to his position in front of me. "Eden, I'm sorry to hear all of that. Nonetheless, I refuse to support your idea to lose in the Trials. Your mother would never forgive me."

"My mother? How is it all of you here know her and I don't?" My eyes narrowed at this news.

"I'm not sure that it is my place to say, Eden."

"Whose place is it to say then? Because I'm getting pretty sick and tired of everyone I meet here bringing her up just to elaborate on nothing."

"Later," He said, winding his milky hands around my own. As much as I disliked it, the touch was calming. "For now, we have a gathering to attend. Shall we?"

Scott lifted an elbow for me to hook my arm through. Just before doing so, I realized that Ellie hadn't given me a choice of shoes. Scott elevated a dark eyebrow at me as I pushed on my muddy sneakers.

"It should be okay, right? The dress will cover them."

He vaguely pointed to the opposite side of the room and opened his mouth to speak but decided against it and extended his elbow again.

The castle had taken on an entirely new look in the daytime. The vast corridors were adorned with stunning artwork and carpeting that spread over the grey, impeccable stone masonry. I was glad that Scott seemed to know where to go and kept my arm locked tightly in his, considering that he might be the only person in the entire building with my best interest in mind. He steered us down numerous hallways as I reveled in the profoundly rich colors surrounding us, ranging from lovely sky-blues to inky black.

"So, how has your first trip to our realm been?"

"Well," I chortled, considering the question.

"So far, I've been assaulted by a Demon and transported into captivity. I was manhandled by the prince last night-"

"I'm sorry?" Scott halted so abruptly that I nearly tripped over my own feet.

"He did what?"

"No, not like that," I shook my head. "I lipped off to him, and he had to assert his dominance."

Scott looked at me through narrowed eyes. His jaw tensed and relaxed in rhythm to his fingers, tapping my arm. He was obviously not thrilled about the bit of knowledge I had just shared. Shouldering me to a more shaded area of the hall, he spoke in a low voice, his eyes darting up and down the stretch.

"Eden, listen to me. Blaive is the prince, but he has no right to lay his hands on you." He stopped scanning for guards only long enough to provide me with an attractive, tender smile.

"If something like that happens again, you will let me know, won't you?"

"Uh, yeah, I guess...but--"

"No, don't second guess it. I'm here to help you. Understand?"

I agreed, not knowing what someone like him could do against someone like the prince. Or if I'd even spend time alone with that jerk, Rowan, a second time. Scott beamed at me fondly and yanked me into the hall just in time for an armed guard to pass through. Scott played off the little treasonous talk like nothing had just been said at all, bowing his head to the guard as we passed.

"What is this meeting, precisely?"

"It is part of the tradition. Blaive will present himself and talk about the kingdom for, well, who knows how long. The elf enjoys talking about himself. We could be there for the rest of the night."

"Great," I grumbled, already prepared to spin around and spend the day in my room.

"Can't we just skip it?"

"How I wish we could!" Scott produced a hearty laugh from deep in his chest. It made me smile, as though we were old buddies. Of course, he was a total stranger, even if he was the only helpful person I'd come into contact within this world. A roaring crowd could be heard the farther we walked. Scott brought us to a halt in front of a large set of doors.

"Remember, the people here are nobility. Speak with respect, no matter how much they might make you want to do otherwise. We are Witches, which means that they all share a common distaste for our kind. It is to be expected, no matter where you go here. Do not give them a reason to validate that prejudice. Alright?"

"No pressure at all..." I said, chewing my cheek.

"I'll be here, don't worry," He said before stretching out a long arm to push open one of the doors.

I swallowed hard, promising myself that I could do this.

Hopefully.

Chapter Seven

THE INTERIOR WAS BUSTLING WITH BODIES.

I gripped Scott's hand tightly against my clammy palm as he guided me. Unfamiliar eyes of all species followed us warily as we moved. Heads swiveled, and people drifted aside so we couldn't brush them. Fine by me, I didn't want to touch them any more than they wanted me to. Scott had been right about them peering down their noses at us.

Head carried high, he accepted it with grace, making me feel small and insignificant with my chin sinking to my chest. Dodging the glares was difficult, but I didn't have to worry about it for long. As soon as Rowan descended on the grand staircase, with a strong hand holding onto the elaborately designed banister, faces turned to give him their full attention. I saw Scott's jaw contract again at the sight of the prince, but I looked elsewhere, not sure of why I felt just as enthusiastic about the prince showing up as everyone else.

"Welcome, everyone!" Rowan's rumbling voice was abnormally powerful. As though there was an unseen microphone being held in front of those full lips of his.

"Thank you to everyone who attended this assemblage, in

support of your chosen individuals who will be competing in the Devotion Trials! I wish to extend an apology for our delayed start. We had a Witch on the loose." A flush filled my cheeks and crept into my ears as the crowd roared with laughter and whispered exchanges, several heads turning to glance at me.

What an asshole.

"Please, drink, eat, and enjoy getting to know each other while you listen to me ramble on." Another chuckle from the people.

"This will be the last day that families are permitted to see their participant. You should have all chosen an individual escort by now. Please make sure that it is decided by midnight, at the latest. As for the Trials, there will be three, as is customary. We must remember that this was designed to bring our strongest, our smartest into the light. Those who fail will lose nobility status as it is recognized by the crown. However, the one who completes the Trials will have proven themselves worthy of marrying me and will be allowed to ascend as Fae-Queen."

"Told you, the elf can't stop himself from showing his power," Scott whispered, prompting a grin to tug at my lips. He smiled too but never turned away from Rowan.

Gleaming red eyes illuminated in the corner of my vision. Expecting to see Harper, I returned the look, but was met with the pretty, angular face of a female. She stood several feet away and was dressed in a revealing two-piece gown that looked more like a bikini with sheer cloth hanging from it. It was ruby-colored, resembling her eyes. I scowled at her smirk that was fixed on her face for no reason that was clear to me.

"...I'm confident that this series of Trials will pull us closer to a resolution during these troublesome times..."

Demon lady drew her sights away from me to get a better listen as Rowan proceeded. I shifted to notice him glancing back at her for a fleeting moment. The recollection of his words from the evening before crossed my thoughts, he had stated that he would only support 'one.' Could he have been speaking of the

Demon, and if so why her in particular? Something pulled at my gut. Could it be jealousy? Surely not.

"What war?" I whispered to Scott. He glanced down at me and then over to the pod of Demons to our right.

"Between the Fae and the Demons." He said quietly with no implication that he would later elaborate.

"In conclusion, I'd like to thank you all once again. It is our pleasure to have so many of you with us for the Devotion Trials. Please, enjoy the rest of the evening!"

Slapping my hands together, I joined the applause and waited as the various groups tore apart and restarted their chatting. Several factions worked their way to the base of the staircase and Rowan was lost in the mass of bodies.

"Excuse me for a moment, Eden," Scott said and released my hand before I could argue. *Great.* I was a lone rabbit amongst a pack of wolves and hadn't the slightest clue how to converse with those creatures. The only thing I could think to do was find Rowan, and perhaps get some more information seeing as how Demon princess, and her creepy stare, had caused me to miss a chunk of his speech.

Working my way around in the general direction I had last seen him, I was extra careful not to make eye contact with anyone. Peering on tiptoes over the sea of heads, I could just make out the dark curls stretching above the crowd. I accelerated, weaving between the mob with a growing urgency to get away from them all. Just a few more steps...

Exactly as I was preparing my mouth to call to the prince, a woman with long inky locks overlaid with a sheer black veil took a step back just as I stepped forward. She twisted around just as I came hurtling into her rooted frame. The impact cast me onto my rear in front of everyone. She hoisted the veil from her sharp-featured face, her silver eyes peered down at me through thick lashes. Pointed black eyeliner rimmed her alien eyes, her dark eyebrows held the image of tranquility as her sanguine lips stretched into a snarl.

My stomach lurched like it was trying to escape my abdomen at the display of two razor-sharp fangs alongside her pearly teeth. *Vampire*, my mind instantly shrieked. Thankfully, I was too astonished to vocalize the word. Her smooth, marble-like skin dropped back into a stoic expression as she recalled that there were hundreds of eyes watching our every move.

My neck prickled with the certainty that, had we been alone, she would have drained me of my blood for the mishap. A hush fell across the hall as I eased myself back onto my feet. The woman glanced down at my now-exposed sneakers and produced a burst of piercing laughter, in a sound that seemed about as sweet as a lemon.

"The Coven isn't doing well lately, I see." She sneered in a thickly accented voice.

"Go suck a neck, Lavinia," Scott said from just to my left, making me jump. I hadn't seen him arrive at my side.

"Are you offering?" She asked with glowing eyes.

"Don't you just wish?"

"Hah!" Her laugh rang out again.

"Not even if I were starving would I drink your filthy blood, Witch."

"So everyone wins!" I exclaimed with a bit more zeal than intended.

Scott seized my hand and dragged me away from the growing murmurs. As we moved, the crowd erupted into gossip and laughter. Never, in my life, had I craved to be alone more than at that moment. Maybe Scott had sensed it because we were headed to a corner that seemed empty. We almost made it, before the Demon woman forced her way in front of us.

"For fuck's sake," I muttered at the ground. Scott jammed an elbow into my ribs, reminding me that I was supposed to behave myself. Right, like he had done when he had challenged the arrogant Vampire.

"Ouch! Sorry...Nice to meet you, my name is Eden."

"Nija." She replied the amused smile once again on her lips.

"Quite dense one would have to be, to walk directly into a Vampire. You came from the mortal realm. Is that a normal behavior for your kind, to be so obviously simple?"

"Yes," I snapped. How did she know where I came from?

"Back on earth, walking into people is what we strive for."

"No need to get irritated," Nija settled her large, indigo fingernails against her breast, pretending to be hurt by the response.

"How would I know what humans do? I don't associate with your kind."

Her eyes flicked between Scott and me.

"In the mortal realm or otherwise." She added.

With her other hand, Nija reached out to stop a passing female with moss-green hair. The woman's huge, earthy eyes peered at her in puzzlement.

"Kariye, what do you make of the idea of Witches being able to compete?"

"Oh, I don't know, Nija," The girl gave me a grimace that I'm pretty sure was meant to be a smile. It didn't come off that way, she rather looked like she was in discomfort. Nija glowered at the girl and shook her head, sending her cropped, violet hair around her shoulders in tumbles. I took note that there were no horns visible on her head, though her glowing red eyes were a dead giveaway that she was a Demon.

"Moron."

"What is your problem?"

"My problem is none of your concern, hag."

The heat was once again rising in my throat, this one of anger. I could sense it scorching its way around my innards.

"Eden, stop. Walk away." Scott hissed. Turning to look at him, fully ready to slap him as well, my gaze fell to the direction of his pointed finger. He was motioning to my hands, which were exhibiting what looked to be magma flowing in my veins. I swung them behind my back and avoided Nija's hate-filled eyes.

"Yes, step away before you do anything you'll regret, little Witch."

Who was she calling little at nearly the same height as myself? Harper had called me the same thing, maybe it was a Demon thing. The warmth of my power lingered, coursing within my veins, making me want to show Nija how strong I could be. What I did, instead, was stick out my tongue like an upset child and spin on my heel to move elsewhere.

"You can't do that here, do you want to be arrested?" Scott ridiculed under his breath.

"It's not like I was trying. I have no idea how to control this, Scott."

"Merely strive to manage your temper, that's a start. Deep breaths."

"Right."

In through the nose and out through the mouth, I breathed like he recommended. It helped, which enabled me to be presented, by Scott, to the rest of my opponents.

"You've met Nija the Demon, Kariye the Nymph, and Lavinia, who is a Vampire. Let's get you introduced to the rest of them."

He continued to guide me around the hall, where I met the remaining three. First up was a feathered woman, or a harpy as he called her, named Sephial. She did nothing to greet me, only gazed down from two feet above me with her swirling, kaleidoscopic eyes that paired her massive wings beautifully. There was no objection from me when we left after the name exchange.

Next up came the most graceful and attractive woman I had ever seen in my life. She was an elf, and not the kind that helps the fat man make gifts for kids. The tall, slender, looked like she was made of porcelain kind. Her silvery braids fell to her hips, with not so much as a single hair out of place. Irises of smoky gray charmed me as I introduced myself. She dipped her refined head in return with sharp ears peeking out from under her impressive mane. With the chiming voice of an angel, she introduced herself.

"My name is Shael Nueovas, I am of the Fae kingdom. It is a pleasure to meet you, Eden."

Astounded that there was another polite being in this place, I grinned and returned the bow before advancing to the last person. At first glance, I almost believed her to be Ava, with her cascading blonde hair. As she whirled to face me, my heart dropped a touch.

"Eden! Finally, I'm getting a turn to speak with you! I'm Pimea, and the second most hated woman in the palace, well, hated by the other women..."

"Err," I looked to Scott who had fastened his sights on the stunning woman.

"Why is that, exactly?"

"I'm a siren." She said matter-of-factly as if I was supposed to know what that signified.

"Like, a Mermaid?"

"Some call us that, and you can if you'd prefer."

I rolled my eyes away from Scott. Great, even my only friend here so far was captivated by my competition.

"Don't despair, he's not to blame. I tend to have that influence over men." Pimea surprised me with the comment. Wait, could they read minds here?

"My strength is only to influence and attract men. However, Lord Blaive has the power to protect himself from my control, as most of his kind can. So, I'm essentially useless in this competition." She chuckled.

"That makes two of us. I don't know how to control my powers, or even how to summon them."

Pimea looked taken aback.

"You're Mistress Tamora's daughter, how is that possible?"

"You two can resume this discussion later, yes? I need food in my belly, and I'm sure Eden does as well." Scott appeared to have snapped out of Pimea's trance.

"Later," I promised with a bow to Pimea. She returned the gesture and waved before turning to return to her aimless charming.

"I liked that one," I said, following Scott to the abundant meal tables.

"Me too, though not of my own wishing."

I giggled and studied the spread. We had been there for hours, and my late breakfast wasn't holding up against the time. Touching my abdomen, my belly growled in response. Spices filled the air with a wonderful aroma that drew me in like a kid in a candy store. My eyes were alight as they wandered over the golden roast hen, towers of sweet cakes dripping with honey, spicy peppered potatoes, and everything else one could imagine.

Scott reached for meat and potatoes while I opted for as many different things as I could fit on a single plate. I'm rather positive that some people were staring, but I didn't care. I was here, why not take advantage of the food that didn't come out of the freezer and get nuked in a microwave? The two of us spotted a secluded table to eat at and I started to stuff my face. Scott grunted in disapproval at my animalistic eating display but proceeded to eat his meal, regardless.

"Maybe I could get used to this place," I said once I had polished off the plate, sinking back with a full belly.

"Well, here's your chance to tell Lord Blaive yourself." Scott stood and excused himself, despite my questioning frown. I turned on the wooden seat and was met with Rowan's dazzling smile.

Chapter Eight

"Your highness," I sighed, not bothering to stand and receive him. The defiance was stinging his ego, I could see it deep in his eyes. Butterflies fluttered around in my belly as I tried to maintain my resistant stare. What was he going to do in front of all these people? Have me arrested?

"Witch." He stated quietly. Okay, that was just hurtful. At least, I think that he had meant it to be taken that way. I happened to be a Witch, so perhaps I shouldn't have been so offended by the term.

"Please, behave appropriately. It wouldn't be very becoming of me to have to show you how to act in front of your rivals."

I almost choked on a gulp of water. Flashes of Rowan's body pressed against my own spread through my mind like flames in a dry barn. As carelessly as I could manage, I sprang from the seat and gave him a clumsy dip. His pale eyes shone as he watched me in amusement. It was humorous for him to see me struggling to fit in. At least now I knew for sure that it bothered him when I acted like I didn't need to follow the rules.

"Here's a crazy idea, send me home. That would teach me a lesson."

He smiled and bent forward, the raw aroma of the forest emanating from his skin. My jaw went slack as I ogled his impeccable grin. He had moved too close, and I had been single for too long to be teased this way. I tore my eyes off of him and fiddled with a jewel that dangled from my dress.

"I'm not sending you anywhere unless you'd like to be shown around the dungeon? All it would take is a single flick of my fingers. Don't test me, Witch. I'm not one to play games with silly girls."

"But you expect girls to play games for you?" I snapped back, wishing Scott would come and throw a hand over my mouth before it got me into real trouble. To locate him, I swiveled my eyes around the room. My wandering gaze was led back with a jolt when Rowan grabbed my chin between finger and thumb and forced me to look into those intense eyes of his.

"When I met you last night, I hated to welcome you here, pitied you even. However, that tongue of yours is making me want to keep you here. Just to spite you."

"You can't do that." I retorted. He couldn't, could he? Where the hell was Scott?

"Try me. I can do anything I wish. Your Coven isn't what it once was, and after the Trials, I will possess an essential ally in this gods-forsaken conflict. With a century-old war put to rest, I could stomp your vile Coven into the ground, and would do so with pleasure."

I started to open my mouth in protest, but no words came out. It was one thing to be sassy, knowing that I was putting myself at risk, but I didn't know anything about the Coven or their numbers. Could he be serious about killing off every single one of them? The hard look in his eyes alongside the tight muscles of jaw told me that he was about as serious as a heart attack. My throat constricted and I felt panic seeping into me.

"Now, be a good Witch, and learn your place."

Without being able to look into his eyes anymore, mine

lowered as I nodded and took a step back with a heavy head. I could feel his seething anger radiating off of him in heatwaves that made me want to start running and never stop. It was the first time since arriving in the Fae realm that I felt like I had been shaken awake. Rowan had jolted me from a dream, only for me to find that I was stuck in the nightmare. Moisture settled in my eyes. I hastily dried them with the back of my wrist. Rowan's harsh stare lingered, full of disgust before he turned to depart.

"Eden, what's wrong?" It was the voice of Pimea. She wrapped an uninvited arm around my shaking arms. Not wanting her to see me weak and crying, I sniffed back my emotions and gave her my best smile.

"It's hard, yes? Coming from the mortal realm? Come, I can get us away from here."

I nodded, wanting nothing more than to get the heck out of that grand hall, I allowed her to pull me aside by the wrist. She was quick on her feet as she moved us through the crowd. I'd be lying if I said it wasn't at least a little fun. Pimea seemed so free, so full of life. Like, losing her noble status wouldn't affect her one bit if she failed these Trials. My curls lashed my face as we ran, like teenagers ditching a school dance under the watchful eyes of the principal.

"This way," She giggled and yanked me through a small service door used by the cuisine staff. Once inside, we made our way through the kitchens being watched by the workers as we passed. My heart raced as I thought about what Rowan had just said to me. What would be the harm in us taking a stroll through the castle, surely someone would have stopped us if we were doing anything that we weren't supposed to, right?

The area smelled of cinnamon and nutmeg which made me regret stuffing myself so full. Pimea continued to drag me until we were well away from the grand hall and back into the winding corridors. Maybe I was out of shape, or maybe she was just fit, but by the end of our sprint I had my hands on my knees as I stood there, gasping for air. She stifled a laugh and helped me back into a walking stance.

"Let's get back to the guest quarters," She said. "We can talk there. The others shouldn't be back for a while yet."

"Okay, just give me a second to catch my breath." I panted.

"Eden!" I rolled my eyes at the sound of Scott's voice. *Busted*.

"Hey, Scott. Before you say anything, I just needed to get out of there. The prince already delivered his speech, I'm sure he won't mind that we left." I swiped a hand through the air dismissively.

"I'm not bothered about you leaving. I couldn't find you and was concerned."

He eyed Pimea, being mindful to keep his distance as much as possible while placing a hand on my lower back and meeting my eyes with his. She crossed her arms and tapped her toes impatiently.

"We were going to have girl talk."

"That can wait a moment, would you mind..."

He shooed her with a wave of his fingers. Pimea threw her head back and slapped her palms against her thighs before making her way further down the corridor to allow us a moment. With a brow slanted in great disapproval, Scott made sure the coast was clear before starting in on me.

"I'm sorry I left you with Lord Blaive back there, I can't stand to be around the man. I supposed he wouldn't try anything with an audience. He didn't, did he?"

"No," I shook my head and wiped the sweat from my brow, not caring if he was looking.

"So, you only left to have a chat with the siren?" His piercing azure gaze sliced through me like a knife, he was not buying it.

"Okay, fine. I might have aggravated Rowan-"

"Lord Rowan!" Pimea shouted from down the hall. Scott sighed, and his eyes rolled to the back of his head as he drew his fingers through his silky hair at the scalp. With a firm grip, he pulled me further out of earshot. I jerked my wrist from his hold with a scowl.

"Proceed."

"I didn't mean anything by not standing and bowing, I just don't like him-"

"Eden. What did he do?"

I was beginning to see that tiptoeing around the subject would get me nowhere. With outstretched arms, I attempted a show of peace before sharing whatever I had provoked.

"He may have threatened me a little. And maybe it wasn't just a little, or just me..."

"Tell me, please."

"He said he could stomp your Coven-"

"Our Coven."

"Okay. Are you going to keep doing that? Because if you are..." I sighed and dug underneath my fingernails, an old nervous habit. Scott waited for me to finish.

"He said he could stomp our Coven into the ground if I don't behave myself here."

"Are you going to? Behave that is."

"Yes. I don't worry if I get under his skin, but I would never intentionally put other lives in harm's way."

He cocked a brow in surprise.

"What?"

"Well, I don't think it would be a bad idea for you to stand up for yourself. Look, Eden, we Witches have been swept under the rug for decades, centuries even. There have been few bold enough to show a backbone in the face of danger. Besides," He smiled and tucked a damp curl behind my ear. I leaned in, just ever so slightly, to his soothing touch. He held my stare as he spoke, sending ripples of feel-good sensations all over me.

"You alone are stronger than the entirety of that grand hall in union. There is a reason they hate us, Eden. It is out of fear."

Trailing a finger over my chin and across my lips, he studied every tiny reaction I had to his caress. Exerting a stride backward, I shook the warm feeling away and gave him a phony smile. His fingers remained in the space between us for a few seconds before descending to his side.

"I'm sorry, it's just that Pimea is waiting for me. We will talk more another time, okay?"

"Of course."

He twisted away, and a sting of guilt stabbed my gut. Without another word, I retreated to my newest companion. She was standing, hand on hip, scrutinizing the artwork on the walls. Catching my footsteps thudding down the hall, she turned, and a smile spread from ear to ear.

"Finally!"

Together we initiated our trip back to her room. I peered over my shoulder to find that Scott had disappeared. He was too good at doing that. It hurt just a little to know that, this time, it was my fault. Why did I just flake out like that without an explanation? Just the same as when I had left Ben at the bar without a word. The fear of letting my guard down.

Pimea stopped us beside the door with the Celtic knot before I realized how far we had walked in silence. I laid a hand on the door and was rewarded with a searing zap to the palm.

"Ow!" I jerked back and clutched the wrist of my aching hand in horror. Pimea chuckled and placed her hand upon it, ramming it open.

"You can't open your opponent's bedroom doors, it's a rule."

"I-I'm sorry," I stuttered. "I thought this one was mine, it has the same symbol on the door."

"They all have that, it's a sign of unity. Maybe they are hoping that the ones who lose will remember it once they have to relinquish their authority. And the crown wonders why there is a war going on when things like this silly Trial happen every so often."

The siren swept an arm through the doorway, permitting me to enter first. Her room looked very similar to my own, save for the enormous tank sitting in the place of a bed. Aquamarine seawater filled the tank, and a gentle swirl disturbed it, sending the slightest ripples to the surface.

"I can walk like a human, I can eat like a human, but I cannot sleep like one. They had the water specially transported from my home-sea. I do miss home, especially once inside of that box. It is the water of my people, but I don't have the privilege of swimming freely in it."

"I'm so sorry, that must be awful."

Pimea shrugged her delicate shoulders and motioned to the table and chairs set.

"Shall we?"

I sat with her, respectfully declining a bowl of grapes that she pushed across the tabletop in offering.

"So, you don't have your mother's power?" She asked, popping one of the sweet fruits between her plump lips. *Guess we were jumping right into the heavy stuff.*

"I do, I think. I'm just not sure how to use it. Not yet, anyway."

"It will come, in time. And with such a gorgeous teacher... You won't be missing any classes, right? I mean, he is gorgeous, as are you. I almost believed you were Fae when I saw you during our introductions." She smiled with perfectly straight, white teeth.

"Sure," I laughed awkwardly.

"I have an important question to ask you if you don't mind."

She gestured for me to continue while still chewing on the grapes.

"Why do I need my powers for the Trials? I mean, I know now that we aren't going to be killing each other, so why is it important?"

"Even those of us who have always lived with the Fae don't know much about the first two Trials. But what we do know, is that the last one is combat. Not to the death, that would lead to dangerous circumstances between the different kingdoms. It is just a show of strength, proving who is the most suitable to be named queen."

"Like wrestling?" I asked. Pimea's shadowy lashes swept up, and she peeked at me through them.

"You could wrestle, if you'd like. Or you can use your powers. There will be preservation spells cast to protect the competitors from dying."

"What will you use?"

"I don't worry about it these things as I won't make it through to the last round of Trials."

"Why do you say that Pim? You might."

She smirked at the nickname like it was a generous gift I had just offered her.

"I don't care if I drop out as soon as the first horn sounds. Some of our species don't care about things like social status. Especially not as much as the elves and the Demons. And how they do love a good war, to show who cares more."

"The war..." I had forgotten to ask about it.

"Why did it start?"

"Why do most wars start? Resources, power, estranged lovers. This is no different. Lord Rowan's father was alive for the start of this one. He fought on the battleground alongside his only son many times."

"Wait." I laughed nervously, thinking she had misspoken, and drilled her with my eyes. "Lord Rowan can't be older than, what, twenty-six?"

Pimea nearly spit grape flecks all over my face. Throwing a hand over her mouth she quickly cleaned the mess from her chin and eyed me.

"Eden, Lord Blaive is over a century, in years."

"No way."

"I'm guessing human lifespans are much different than ours? Here in the Fae realm we can live for centuries, with the right care. Sometimes spells help too. I believe that Lord Blaive will be celebrating his one hundred and twenty-fifth birthday soon."

"Wow. He looks excellent for his age." I joked, to keep myself from overthinking this whole age thing. We both erupted into laughter. Wiping tears from my cheeks, I beamed at my new friend.

"Thank you, Pimea."

"For what?"

"For being kind to me. I don't get that a lot, especially around here. I appreciate it more than you can imagine."

I departed from the seat, deciding it was about bedtime. I could hear the sounds of people hobbling in intoxicated steps through the halls just outside of the door. Pimea stood to walk me out. Just before she opened the door, I said something that I wasn't sure was fair to ask of her.

"Do me a favor? Don't lose the Trials. Not on purpose anyway. Kick ass and take names, don't let these jerks make you feel like you are less than what you really are."

A crinkle formed at the corners of her eyes as she smiled with her entire face. She flung her arms around my collar and squeezed with more strength than I thought she could produce.

"I will agree to that, so long as you do the same."

"Deal." I accepted.

She pulled back and I could have sworn there was a tear in her eye.

"You know, for a Witch, you aren't that evil."

"Neither are you for a cold-blooded, man-killer." She laughed at that.

I waved goodbye and started to look for my room, marked with the colors of my Coven, green, and gold. Half expecting to get shocked again, once I found it, I pushed it open gingerly. The door swung ajar allowing me to get inside, shut it, and search through the wardrobe for clean pajamas. I carefully pulled the strings of the corset back loose and removed the dress, hanging it over the back of a chair.

Finding a fresh nightgown, I kicked off my shoes and pulled it over my head before crawling into bed. The crackling of the hearth aided in relaxing my mind and body. Just as I was about to drift off, an image of Ava, shouting at me the day I had left, invaded my thoughts. I questioned how she was doing without me, how my father's health was holding up.

The good sensations I had established when chatting with Pimea were put to rest in an instant. I was overwhelmed with a dread that ran deep, entering my soul. Hazel eyes that matched our father's stared at me from behind my eyelids, pushing me to keep going.

A new concept hit me like a slap in the face. Did my father know about this place and what my mother was? Surely not, I convinced myself and rolled onto my side. Sinking into the fluff that made up the bed, I breathed a sigh and let sleep overcome me.

Chapter Nine

"Get up sleepyhead," Scott said, rocking my shoulder. I growled at him and rolled to my other side, as far from him as possible.

"Come on, Eden. We have lessons that start today. The sooner we begin, the better. You're going to need every second of it to learn your spells and alchemy."

"Is it common for people to come into your room and bother you while you are sleeping here?" I snapped, my speech was muffled by the pillow.

I felt the bed jostle as he sat himself down on the edge of it. I sighed and elevated my head, fairly certain that if I didn't show some signs of life, he would wait there forever. I was pretty positive that my hair was a mess, and that my makeup from the day before was most likely smudged to hell as I glowered at him through bloodshot eyes.

"Good morning," He smiled.

"Do you have coffee in this realm? Or do you all expect me to make it through every day without a drop of caffeine?"

The smell of spices filled the room making my belly gurgle. Ellie, who just happened to be setting the table with mountains of the same foods I had eaten the morning before, rushed to the door with the new information.

"I'll get that drink to you right away, miss!"

"No, that's-"

She was already gone. Secretly, I was glad. The fragrance of coffee alone might be enough to motivate me to make it through the day at this point. Without warning, Scott clutched my wrist and began to pull me from under the covers. I'm not sure why I reacted the way I did, but it presumably had something to do with the caffeine deficiency.

With a swift yank backward, I brought him, and myself, tumbling over the side of the mattress. The whole thing might have even been comical, had he not landed directly on top of me with his thighs between mine. I could feel every fragment of his sensual heat as it radiated from his body and all over mine. Azure eyes bore into me. He studied my face from my eyes, to my chin, and back up. His stare dwelled on my lips.

Before I could shove him off of me, or at least attempt to, his head dipped toward me. The picture of Rowan's body flush against mine ran through my mind and I twisted my head away just in time for his lips to make contact with my jaw. Holding his forehead against my temple, he withdrew his kiss and squeezed his eyelids shut.

"I-I apologize, Eden, I don't know what came over me."

"It's okay." I lied.

"Please pardon my being so presumptuous," He leaned back and moved a foot beside my waist to stretch himself into a half-standing, half-bowing position. I took the hand he extended and let him haul me to my feet. A hush settled between us. Walking around me, he moved to the wardrobe to sift through it.

"I'm going to eat," I said without needing to and made my way to the table to do just that. I avoided looking straight at Scott. Instead, I concentrated on whatever he was preparing as he extracted a pair of pants, a murky green and gold top, and a thick belt. He then stepped to the chest and yanked it wide open to retrieve a pair of knee-high boots.

"So you don't have to keep wearing those revolting sneakers," He smiled a little and dumped them alongside the garments. Ellie burst through the door just then, nearly making me jump out of my skin, and bustled to the table with a platter in hand. The strong aroma of just-brewed coffee floated around me.

"Oh, thank you so much, Ellie!"

"Of course, miss. Now, we have fresh cream, sugar, and a collection of flavorings if you'd like?"

"I'll take it plain."

Not that I usually drank my coffee black, I just hadn't had any in two days and needed it in my mouth as quickly as possible. Ellie nodded and began to fill a cup that looked like it had been carved from bone. Once she had finished, she assembled the gleaming silver tray amidst the food. With a bow, Ellie left the room. Scott migrated to the door behind her.

"I'll see you in a bit."

"Mmhm."

I didn't watch him leave but instead focused my attention on downing the drink so that I could start on eating my breakfast. Swallowing food by the mouthful until I had my fill, I advanced to the vanity to freshen up before getting dressed. My hair sat in a mass of knots at my nape. After brushing through it vigorously and removing the pins Ellie had expertly arranged in it the night before, I pulled it into a long French braid. When I had finished with that, I washed the remaining makeup away with the fresh water and cloth. Once I was satisfied with my appearance, I began to pull on the garb left for me. First came the simple pants that hit at my hips and fit me like a pair of tights.

Next up was the tunic, which I examined before pulling over my head. The embroideries embellishing the neckline had me convinced that the glistening thread was formed from genuine gold. It felt heavy and snug against my breasts as I dragged it down past my hips and looped the belt around my waist. I looked like a female Robin Hood. Which was sort of cool, in my opinion.

Pushing the boots onto my feet, I was delighted to see that they fit perfectly. I fastened them and crammed one last spoonful of eggs into my mouth before leaving the room. The passageway was chock-full of people, probably family members of those who had them, who were departing the castle. Disregarding the frowns aimed at me, I searched to find anyone who could tell me how to find wherever the heck I was supposed to be going.

Scott was resting against a wall just a few doors down from mine. I figured that he had probably decided, once leaving my chamber, that I wouldn't be able to make my way around the castle without a guide. Ignoring the memory of what had transpired just a short while ago, I made my way over to him. Looking at me from head to toe, he shoved away from the wall.

"What do you think?"

"You look incredible, as always. Now, are you eager to learn your spells?"

Detesting the blush tickling its way up my neck at his praise, I shot him a thumbs up. Without another word, he pivoted and started walking down the hall. I followed at his heels, not wanting to get lost in the chaos of mythological creatures that filled the place from top to bottom.

Scott led us to a rather large, oblong room that was practically empty. It resembled an attic, with a half of an inch of dust covering everything within it. Flush against the walls stood elegantly carved antique bookshelves that were supplied with thousands of books. The other thing in the space that didn't look older than dirt was the enormous table that had been placed in the far right corner of the chamber. Upon it was a variety of bottles and vials packed with different herbs and other things that I didn't recognize. With just a few steps, I approached the table and bent down for a better look.

"Don't touch those just yet," Scott called to me.

"I wasn't!" I yanked back my pointer finger just before it could rap against the glass of a container filled with a mysterious silvery liquid.

"Get over here, I have something to show you."

"Yes, sir." I quipped and stepped to the tall book stand where Scott stood. On top of it rested a heavy, worn book with discolored pages. The binding had been stained a dark lavender, and a symbol was branded into the center of the cover. I traced my finger along the swirling design and felt a tug inside of me, as though my soul was beckoning the book, inviting it in.

"It's beautiful," I said in a voice just above a whisper.

"Not just beautiful," Scott planted his fist on the symbol. With eyes shut, he murmured foreign words through his teeth, ones that I didn't understand. A prism of color burst across the symbol like a swirling rainbow. With now-open eyes and a flash of a grin in my direction, Scott swept through the pages.

"This is our Book of Shadows; our Coven's book of spells, alchemy, and notes from long before our time." His blue eyes were alight as he peered up at me. "Before your mother's time, Eden."

"Did she write in it?" I asked. The excitement in my voice made me want to kick myself. She had abandoned us, I shouldn't care if she scribbled in a dusty old book. Yet, I did. Every fiber of my being desired to tear the book from Scott's fingertips, just to get a better look. This was my history, the parts I didn't know about. I hungered for it.

"We have all contributed to the book, well, all of us except–"

"Me," I concluded.

He briefly planted a hand on my shoulder before stepping away and allowing me the chance to view it in my own time. The pages felt warm beneath my fingertips like they were alive. Odd as it was, it felt good to hold. It felt like energy. Like power.

"What are these spells for?"

"Everything you could possibly think of. Page twenty-nine is a sleeping spell, page one-hundred and twelve is a spell to aid in refreshing day-old fish, page three hundred and nine is," He paused to swallow and glance at my lips. "A love spell."

I made sure to hurry past that one immediately, so as not to see a single word of it.

"Have you ever used them?" I asked without looking at him.

"Of course. There are simple spells that can be used every day. Just as there are spells that can only be used every few years. But I think that's enough of the book for now, let's try and work out the physical material first."

He slammed the book shut and moved to an empty area of the massive room, planting his feet at hip-distance apart. I stepped away from the stand and moved to his side.

"To begin manifesting the power inside, you need to think of something that uproots you on an emotional level. Fill that void thirsting within you and drive it into a solid form. Center that focal point within your chest first, then let it flow through you as naturally as the blood within your veins."

He said it so casually, but I knew it was much simpler said than done. Closing my eyes, I attempted to do as he had asked of me. The first thing I thought of was Harper attacking me in the alleyway. Then, the fear I felt when he broke into my house and threatened to take Ava away. A hint of a spark ignited inside me. Advancing further, I took a deep breath and reflected on Ava, shouting at me before storming out of the house. Our father was dying and I had been ready to leave her to tend to him all on her own. I remembered the grimace on my father's ashen face as he sat on his hospital bed while nurses poked at him like a pin cushion.

"That's it, Eden," Scott said in a low tone. "I can sense your power stirring within, but you need to push yourself harder. Think of something that hurt you more than anything."

With my eyebrows strained tightly together, I picked through my memories, landing in a spot further back than I had gone in years.

Crimson hair, short and flawlessly styled, hung around her shoulders. The woman was tall and slender. She was kissing my father on the forehead as she handed him a plate full of spaghetti. Turning to me, she beamed as I played with dolls. My stubby fingers reached for her but she held up a finger.

"Just one second sweetheart, Avangeline is crying."

My mother picked up a baby with fat cheeks and wide, hazel eyes that were overflowing with tears. She tousled the baby's bright red curls and cooed to her. Ava smiled, happy once more, as she pinched my mother's cheeks with a delighted squall. Mother laughed and put Ava back in her crib before returning to sit across from me, cross-legged.

I smiled at her, looking deeply into her matching cerulean eyes.

"What did you need, my love?"

"Play with me, Mommy!"

"Alright," She chuckled in a melodic voice. We played together until bedtime. After she had tucked me in, singing something I had long forgotten, the vision leaped forward. An eleven-year-old me was in our living room. Mom and Dad had been arguing all evening. I remembered covering Ava's ears until she had fallen asleep.

"I have to go, Tom, I can't explain why, I just do."

"And what about the kids, Tammy? You're gonna leave them? What the hell is wrong with you, those girls adore you and I--" My father's voice broke.

"I love you too, my darling, and I want to stay more than anything. But another responsibility calls to me, one that I can't ignore." My mother was crying then as well.

"And your responsibility to your children?"

"It will have to wait, I'm afraid. It won't be forever though, Tom. Maybe a year, but it could be much less than that."

"I am begging you, hon, don't do this. Don't leave us. What will I tell them, our girls?"

I watched my mother move across the kitchen to embrace my father as he wept into his palms. It was the first time I'd ever seen him cry.

I felt a tear rolling down my face. Then another, until they began to pool along my neckline. The spark inside was catching fire as I recalled what was happening. This scene had played in my mind too many times throughout my life.

"I love you. Take care of them, won't you, Tom?"

My father looked up at her, denial covering his face. She kissed him between his sobs. Tearing away, she hurried into the living room and met my eyes. My mother rushed to place a kiss on my forehead and pull my head tightly against her bosom. I threw my arms around her waist and held onto her skirt. Breathing her in, I didn't know that this would be that last time I smelled her lavender-scented body wash.

"Take care of Ava. She will need you to be strong, okay baby?"

I nodded and clung onto her skirt until it was extracted from my fingertips as she pulled away and marched through the door, disappearing from our lives forever.

"Eden?" Scott called, pulling me from the memory. My shaking hands darted to my slick face that was wet with tears. The spark burst into full-blown flames inside of me, searing the underside of my skin, trying to dig its way to the surface. I didn't hear the cry as it left my throat. All I could perceive were the flames as they scattered beneath my skin.

With everything I could muster, I forced the shards of power together. They traveled their way through my knuckles and down to my fingertips. Opening my eyes, I watched as the fire burst from my fingers, saturating my hands in emerald flames.

"Wow," Scott breathed. Pulling himself together, he tried to concentrate on guiding me through the rest of it.

"Now, focus on something and let all of that pain go. You can do this, Eden."

Glancing at a stack of books beside a dusty old chair leg, I twisted my body to face it and pulled back before pushing farther forward, shoving my power out of me with all of my strength. I felt the sobbing in my throat turn to something that sounded more like a war cry. Tears gushed across my cheeks and plopped onto my chest. The flames curved into orbs that hovered in front of my palms before shooting outward, and straight into the books. The stack all but disintegrated before us as I collapsed onto my knees.

"Are you alright?" Scott raced to me, stooping to meet me at eye level.

"I'll be fine."

With a sniffle, I wiped my nose with the back of my hand. Scott put his fingers around my elbows and brought me back to my feet.

"Was it about your mother?"

"Yes," I replied through trembling lips. Glancing into his eyes, I knew he felt for me, which just made me feel even more ridiculous. I decided that I didn't care how he viewed me and let my head fall against his firm chest. Once the tears had subsided, and I felt like I could speak in a steady voice again, I pulled away. A thought occurred to me, one that I hadn't thought to ask before. It was a concept that carried a chill deep into my bones.

"Scott?"

"Hmm?"

"Harper, the Demon that collected me, he said that if I hadn't come, they would have brought Ava in my place. Does that mean she is a Witch too?"

"We don't know yet, Eden. We knew that you were because you've been here before, unlike your half-sister."

"Wait, what?" The room started to go all funny. It wavered and wobbled while I stretched my hands out in every direction, searching for something to sit on. Scott caught my arm to stabilize me. With an intense twisting my stomach, I looked up at Scott.

"I assumed you knew, sorry."

"My half-sister? I've been here before?" Saying it felt foreign, wrong. But something about Scott's tone told me it was true. That meant...

"So my father?"

"He is still your father, with or without sharing your blood, he raised you."

"All these years... Why didn't he tell me? And the Coven, where the hell have you been?"

"Eden, it was Tamora's wish that we didn't inform you. The Coven wanted to reach out to you, but we knew that we had to consider your mother and what she felt was best for you."

"I need to get out of here," I said suddenly, throwing a hand over my mouth to stop the vomit building in my throat. I shoved away from him and ran. As fast and as far as I could. Through halls and rooms, I didn't let my feet falter until I had arrived in the blinding sunlight outside of the castle. The guard shouted something as I flew down the steps but I didn't care, I wanted to get the hell out.

I could see from a distance that the passage leading into the city beyond had been shut tight. With a swivel of my head, I searched desperately for somewhere, anywhere, to go. My fingernails dug into my palms as I squeezed them in anticipation when I spotted a hedged that had been trimmed into the shape of an archway. That will do. Keeping my feet at a steady pace, I raced through it and into a clearing. Perfectly clipped bushes lined it in a half-moon shape. I also noticed an enormous water fountain that was spitting water into the air right at the center.

I didn't have time to rest as I detected the guard's heavy armor clanking behind me, they were probably thinking that I was trying to escape. They wouldn't be far off, I just wanted to be far away from there, as quickly as possible. Fuck the Trials. And fuck the asshole hosting them. I wanted to get back to my world, to pretend like I hadn't seen or heard anything here. I'd be good, playing pretend as I allowed my father to take his last breaths without the added stress of knowing what I had learned in my short time here.

I slammed into a gleaming, silver gate that seemed to be there more for decorative purposes than anything. Wrapping my finger around it, I gave the thing a shove, it quickly became apparent that the way was locked tight. A glance over my shoulder told me I had about five seconds to make a choice. Good thing I hadn't been required to wear a dress that day, otherwise I wouldn't have been able to hoist myself over it as easily as I managed to. The adrenaline pumping through my body probably didn't hurt either.

Over the gate was another clearing, this one seemed a tad larger and held the same type of fountain as the other. *Well, aren't we just fancy?* Regardless of how charming it was, I despised every stupid square foot of it. My feet slowed to a halt as I cast a look over both of my shoulders, trying to locate my next route. To the far eastern side lay what looked like a gardening shed. Beyond that, I could see nothing more than another one of the half-moon gardens. How many times could I jump over fences today?

"Halt!" Yelled a guard from twenty feet behind me. His fierce tone ignited a fire in my bum, causing me to spring back into action. I didn't turn to look as I took off in another mad dash. I was headed for the gate and, once reaching it, leaped over it without hesitation. I knew I could keep going for a while amidst the danger that was close at my heels but wondered with uncertainty if I'd be thrown into the dungeons for this. Let them do it, maybe my being a handful will convince Rowan that I need to go home, instead of messing with his pretty picture here.

With another look behind me, I believed that I was finally losing them. No sparkle of gold armor caught the sun's beams as I advanced. With a sigh of relief, I directed my gaze forward once more so that I could see where I was going. Before I could get my head fully back in place, I smashed against something. Hard. Sprawling back like a dead spider, with my limbs flinging up in front of me, I smashed into the ground. The air was forced from my lungs as I crumbled against the grass.

"Shit," I squeaked between teeth that were tightly clenched together. Looking up, I expected to see another fountain, maybe even a nice, stone birdbath. But no, it had to be the one thing that I wanted to discover the least in the world. *Him*.

"Out for a stroll in my gardens?" Rowan asked, flashing me an amused smirk. My lungs nearly seized with the first deep breath I was able to draw in. The feeling of air inflating them sent me into a coughing spell, one that took me a solid three minutes to get under control. Looking up at Rowan through watering eyes, I saw that he held an expression of absolute revulsion across his face. I wasn't sure whether to try and stand and make a bigger fool of myself or to use what Scott had just taught me, to erase this jerk from the face of the planet.

"Something like that," I managed to say while pushing a palm against the soft, perfectly lush grass to restore myself into a standing position. Rowan didn't move to help as I did so. He just stood there, gawking, while I fought to right myself. I knew the pain radiating through me at the moment was plain as day on my face. I hated that he could see it, even though it was out of my control.

Once I had finally found my way back to my feet, Rowan's seafoam stare moved to somewhere over my shoulder. With a prompt movement of his hand, he sent the guards, who had nearly caught up to me, away. Oh, so now I wasn't a threat. Kind of a change in tune after he had twisted me like a pretzel two nights ago.

"Don't you need them? You know, to take me to the dungeon?" I panted, wiping away the sweat that was threatening to drip into my eyes. Rowan took several calculated steps around me. He was circling me. As though he were a lion and I was his prey.

"You won't be going to the dungeons today, Witch."

"Ah, but the day is young. How do you know that for sure?"

"You've used your powers recently. I can smell them on you. Lessons going well?" He asked, changing the subject.

"Too well," I grumbled and began clearing the dirt and grass from my backside. Meeting Rowan's eyes, I could see that they had followed my hands and lingered there.

"Hey! Eyes up here, buddy."

Rowan gave me another smirk and held my glare. If I didn't know better, I'd think he was checking me out.

"What are you doing out here, if the lessons are going as well as you say?"

"Taking a break."

"A break?" He snickered. I liked the sound of it. Too much. Shifting away from him, I took a step in the direction that I had just come from. A hand slammed into my waist, propelling me another two steps backward.

"Yes. A break. Now can I get back to it, please?"

Attempting to push my way past him, I crouched beneath his arm and took another step. With a blink, he was right back in front of me, preventing me from going any further.

"What the hell?" I stopped mid-step. The guy had just freaking teleported or something.

"Show me."

"Show you what? Why don't you show me how the fuck you just moved like that?" I hissed, holding a hand up to block out that annoying ball of light in the sky.

"I'll not be showing you anything. I would prefer to observe what you've learned from the other Witch."

"I thought you said that if I so much as twitched wrong, I'd be dead. Now you are asking me to cast fireballs at you?"

"Fireballs, huh?"

I hated the rude, condescending tone that he used with me. It was like he was talking to a child. A child that he hated. If I thought that I could go through the hell of watching my mother leave, for a second time that day, I'd have given him precisely what he had requested. And I would have directed it at his too-perfect face. There was nothing that I wanted more at that moment than for him to disappear, just as the stack of books had.

"I--I--" Damn. "I can't do it again. Not right now."

"And why is that?"

"I just fucking can't, okay? Drop it."

"Touchy, Witch. You would do well to remember who you are talking to and do so quickly. I saw your little display with Lavinia, and the one with Nija too. You're mouthy in a way that should have gotten you killed by now. I'm astonished that it hasn't."

"Yeah, well, back home we don't just kill people for speaking their mind. So why don't you send me back there and let my own people deal with my mouth?"

Closing the distance between us with a single stride, Rowan was pressed against me before I could say another word. I avoided his eyes, which were burning into my skin. Despite not being able to look at him, I held firm in my resistant stance.

"Why have others do what I can easily do myself? Like it or not, for the entirety of the Trials, that sharp little Witch tongue belongs to me and me alone. Now shut your mouth, or I will do it for you."

His heat was permeating through my clothes and onto my flesh. The freshly clean smell of him excited me in ways I couldn't explain, making parts of my body awaken that had been slumbering for far too long. Retreating another step, all I could think about was the need to distance myself from him. *He's the enemy. Not your boyfriend. Pull it together.* He took notice of the spark of desire embedded deep within me and pulled his lips into a grin.

"You're attracted to me. Aren't you, Witch?" He taunted.

"I think the hot weather is getting to your head." I retorted with a scowl.

"Perhaps you're right," He said moving another step toward me, causing me to react with yet another step away. My hand faltered, causing me to blink against the sunlight hitting my eyes. When I opened them, he was gone. It made me shudder to think that he was able to travel at such an inhuman velocity. Taking a cautious step ahead, I felt his hands wrap around my arm just above the elbows. Without a second in between, he yanked me back and against his wall of a body. "Or, perhaps, you just don't want to admit it to yourself."

"Or, *perhaps*," I mocked him through a tightly clamped jaw. "I'm revolted by you, your world, your people, and just don't want to be anywhere near you."

"Is that so?" He growled into my ear, making my knees go all weak and shaky. *Fuck*, I thought, looking around frantically for something to help me out of the situation I had just landed myself in. Curving an arm through my own two, Rowan pulled my body so tightly against himself that I couldn't have broken free with a chainsaw in my hands. With his available arm, he pulled my chin up until I was looking straight above into the clouds that slowly crept toward the horizon. I felt his breath, hot and thick against the skin beneath my ear.

I could feel every inch of his length as he pushed himself firmly against my ass. My traitor of a vagina moistened, and I tried my best to keep a moan that had begun rising in my throat, at bay.

"If I take you as my wife, you won't have a say in my being this close to you. Nor will you be able to control seeing my people in my world. I despise your kind as well, I can assure you that. But under my watch, you wouldn't have room to breathe, let alone use your Witchy spells against the people of this world that you so loath." His tone had gone from seductive to pissed-off real quick.

"I'd sooner throw myself from the top of your castle than to become anything close to being your wife, Lord Blaive." I sneered back at him, terrified of the thought of it alone. With skilled hands, Rowan wrapped my braid into his palm. Pushing his fingers tightly against the hair, he had full control of my head and spun me around to face him. My chin was parallel with the ground, making it so I had to look down my nose to see his eyes, which were alight with anger.

His other arm snaked around my waist and hauled me up

against him. I shoved my hands onto his boulder of a chest and tried my hardest to push myself free. A roguish grin spread across his lips as he watched me struggle. He leaned into me even harder. I wanted to kick him in the balls to get those flawlessly shaped lips away from mine.

"What do you want me to say?" I shouted, fighting the urge to claw his eyes out. "That I'd be happy to marry you? That I'll gladly bear your heirs and--"

"I'm not concerned about anyone bearing my children." He cut in.

Wait, what? When royals married, was it not their first goal to produce more perfect little royal-blooded babies? Maybe he really was just marrying for the benefit of his people. Maybe he was less of a kidnapping monster than I thought he was. Just as the thought crossed my mind, he tugged harder on my braid. *Nope, still an asshole.*

"However, if you do manage to make it through the Trials, which you won't, you will do anything and everything that is expected of you."

"I won't be marrying you, Rowan. I can guarantee that. And if I'm forced to, I will not serve you."

A growl rose from deep inside of his broad chest. I had done it now. I braced myself as I assumed he was about to throw me to the ground. Surely, he would call the guards and have me thrown in the dungeon for the rest of my life. His silky, sweet breath filled my nose. My eyes flew wide open as he crushed his lips upon mine. I wanted to fight it, I really did. But my body didn't get the memo.

Maybe it was out of instinct that I relaxed into his firm, heart-less kiss. His pillowy lips worked against mine in a way that it sent tiny prickles across my skin and provoked me into doing the same. The moisture between my legs increased as we molded to one another, despite my brain screaming that this was a mistake. Rowan's hand drifted down my lower back until he reached my ass, which he took a secure grip of. Just as I was about to give in, to practically beg him to remove his clothes while I did the same with mine, he pulled away.

My lips remained parted as I peered at him from beneath my thick, dark eyelashes. His eyes were cold and unfeeling as he gazed back. *Right*, I almost forgot that we hated each other. This had been nothing more than a warning.

"You already serve me, Witch. And you will do so until I allow you to stop. Think of this moment, the next time you assume that you have any sort of authority here." Rowan removed his hand from my ass and slid it around to the damp area between my legs. Not pressing hard enough to touch my core, his lips twitched. If he had actually pressed hard enough to touch me instead of just my pants, I'd probably have broken loose and asked him to finish the job. With his thick fingers resting on my damp clothing, he leaned in close enough for his nose to brush my own.

"I hardly touched you, and you were already willing to be mine," He said in a gravelly voice that melted me into a puddle.

I'm going to kill him.

"But you needn't worry. You will lose the Trials. Because you are a weak and foolish little Witch."

He untangled my hair from his fingers, allowing me to stumble back. Rowan was right, I knew that, and I hated myself for it. I stared at the ground as he moved away from me, retiring to his previous position of viewing the gardens. Without another look in his direction, I ran from him.

Chapter Ten

Rowan

I OBSERVED HER LOVELY SCARLET HAIR TUMBLING DOWN HER back as she fled. It had slackened from her braid at my own hand. Perhaps I should have gone easier on her, but I hadn't been capable of controlling myself. She was stunning in every way, well, except for the incessantly wagging tongue that she couldn't keep still. Yet, looking at her head fall as I grasped the thick braid in my hand, the way her neck elongated.... gods, she could be my downfall.

I wouldn't let that happen. Nija and her people had made me an offer I simply could not deny. My people cried out for an end to the war, and I was prepared to give it to them, despite what that meant for me. I was a soldier, one of the best at what I did, which was to kill. Half-LightFae or not, my father had driven the instinct into me from birth. And the Witch, as unpredictable as her kind could be, had me in a state of uncertainty that made me want to plunge a dagger straight through her black, dripping heart.

On the other hand, I couldn't block her from my mind.

Which was precisely why I had come to the outer gardens to begin with. I needed space and some fucking silence. Instead, I was met by the very person I had been trying to shake. Worse than that, she had provoked the DarkFae instinct buried inside of me. I wanted her, and not in a tender way. I wanted to rip that tunic to shreds and kiss the luscious, beautiful breasts hiding within it.

Drawing my fingers to my lips, I pulled them in with my tongue, tasting her delicious sexual arousal. My cock pulsated at the memory of her scorching desire. She had wanted me, at least where sex was involved. But I had put her in her place, understanding that the chances of her winning were slim, if any. If she did somehow manage to best Nija, as extraordinary as that would be, she had made it very clear she wouldn't have me.

I could make her if I wanted to. She could be on her knees at my feet in a heartbeat, begging me to fuck her over and over again. I smiled, just thinking about it. The desire to see her beneath those damn clothes was one I would have to satisfy, sooner rather than later if I had it my way.

"Trying to mate with one of the princesses already, my Lord? And before the first Trial has even begun? Tsk, tsk."

Turning to look Nija in her fiery eyes, she smirked as she flounced her way over to me. Her breasts were on display, her nipples only concealed by two strips of red leather. The bitch constantly dressed in red, and not just because it was the color of her house. She had a unique way of inspiring lust, not uncommon for a Demon. It was the same reason she hid her horns, so it would appear less like she wanted to devour your soul that way.

Faekind didn't include Demons, though their powers could be similar. I would know. My mother had been a Demon as well. Nija may not have been a Faery, but she could mind fuck anything she was able to lay those daggers-for-eyes on.

"Good morning to you as well, Nija."

"Having second thoughts about our deal?" She asked, letting

her forked tongue slide seductively across her full bottom lip. She pulled an arm around my waist while using her opposite hand to tug up her skirt until her most delicate parts were on full display. I swallowed hard and attempted to look away before she tugged my chin back to her sharp face.

"Not for a second," I answered through tight lips.

Chapter Eleven

IT WAS MIDDAY IN THE FAE KINGDOM.

I sheltered myself below the covers on my bed, where I had been hiding all day. Scott had come in at some point earlier that morning, trying to convince me that we had lessons that needed learning. I just wasn't feeling it. In fact, I wasn't feeling too much of anything. My emotions were a complete train wreck that had been set on fire and put out with gasoline.

The previous day had been the last straw for me. All I could think about was getting out of this freak show of a world. But I wasn't sure how to do it. I had already taken a candlestick to the window, for real this time, and the glass hadn't so much as cracked. What it did do, however, was send me flying backward, and directly into the bedpost. I flinched as I remembered how that one had felt on my back.

After that, I had crawled into the bed and moped over this unforeseen turn of events that my life had taken me down. Ellie kept coming in to check on me throughout the day and to remind me that I had been ordered to attend a ball that night. A freaking ball. It was every girl's dream, right? Not this girl. I'd rather take my chances in the freaky forest. But first, I needed to get my hands on one of those crystals that Harper had used to make the portal.

A lightbulb illuminated above my head as I realized what I was going to do. Yes, how had I not thought of it before? Maybe I didn't need to be in the forest for it to work. What if I could do it from inside of the castle? *All I need is a little more information, the crystal, and a map leading me directly to Rowan's personal chambers.*

"Mistress, I know that you asked me not to bother you again but the--"

"Ellie, do you know where Ro-err-Lord Blaive's room is located?"

Ellie looked a touch surprised, with her eyes nearing the size of dinner plates as she considered the question. Her tiny finger tapped against her wrist for a few seconds before flinging into the air above her.

"You'd like to thank him personally, for the ball?"

"Yeah, something like that."

She pulled a flimsy, stained piece of parchment from her apron and unfolded it, pointing at a little square. I burned the image of the square into my mind as she folded it back up and handed it over to me.

"That's it right there, you might be able to make it before the ball. That is, if you will finally allow us to prepare you." Her voice was tight, on the verge of irritation.

"Sure," I exhaled a relieved sigh through my smiling lips. "Let's do it."

Ellie happily trotted to the door, pulling it wide open to allow a crowd of creatures just like her to enter. The room became a whirlwind of movement as they started primping and preening me from head to toe. And I do mean that literally. Sitting me at the vanity, they began to pluck my eyebrows. One was swiping blush across my high cheekbones delicately while another filed my fingernails, leaving them in perfect almond shapes.

From the corner of my eye, something sparkled like a disco

ball, sending little flickers of light all over the place. I bent my neck to look at whatever was causing it, despite the angry remarks from one of the little women. I gasped as four of them walked in, each one at a different corner of a huge load of fabric. Standing, I ignored the complaints as I strode to it to get a better look.

Massive was an understatement. This thing was a ball gown and could swallow all of us whole under the billowy skirt. With wide eyes, I trailed my fingers down the glittering gems that lay, expertly placed, against the forest-green fabric. The skirt swayed like sea waves at the slightest hint of movement.

"I would have *killed* to wear this to Prom," I whispered in awe.

"What's that, mistress?" Ellie asked with a smile, not understanding what I was talking about.

"It's sort of like a ball, in the human realm."

"I see. How very exciting. You'd have been the envy of everyone there! Just as you will be tonight, we will make sure of that."

With that, I was hauled back to the vanity for more makeup. With shimmering golden pigment on my eyelids, dark mascara on my lashes, and bright scarlet on my lips, I felt like a movie star. Never before had I seen myself this way, and not for lack of Ava trying to make it happen. It was lovely, not my style, but I certainly wasn't complaining. Especially with the notion that Rowan would be there. Not that I planned on attending.

My stomach erupted into butterflies as I remembered his soft lips pressed against mine.

No, stop it.

To prevent myself from lingering on it, I focused instead on my hair that was being coiled around a hot iron, making my natural curls look less frizzy. When the one working on my hair had finished curling it, she began to weave it into a cascading half-updo. Ellie pushed her aside to finish the job before pulling a corset as tight as possible around my waist. I no longer regretted skipping all of my meals that day, as I'm not sure they would have fit in that corset with me.

The last task was to step into the divine gown. I did so gingerly and allowed the other females to pull it up around me. Once they had done so, I took a second to shove the map in between my pushed-up breasts. Continuing to examine the dress, I noticed that the sleeves were made of the same material as the skirt and hung, like beautiful chandeliers dripping with gems, just off the shoulder. I ran my hands down the delicate fabrics of the dress and smiled, despite my anxiety over what I would be doing in the gown.

"You look just like the Faekind, miss." Ellie beamed, with tears gleaming in her large eyes. I took her hand and squeezed it, noticing that she didn't flinch away from me this time. I liked her. I'd miss her the most, I thought. Her and Pimea, who I hadn't even seen since the first day I met her.

"Thank you, Ellie." I grinned back.

"Well then," She sniffed her tears away loudly and shooed the others with her hands. "We will be off. You have a wonderful time this evening, mistress."

Bowing my head slightly at her, I watched as they left through the door. Taking a second to check myself out in the mirror, I tucked my hair behind one ear and smiled, wishing I had my cell phone so that I could immortalize this moment with a picture. Ava would be proud. Beyond proud, she'd be straight-up jealous that I had an opportunity to go to a ball. I was sure there was some way I could twist this into my lie about being in New York City.

With one last big breath, I walked to the door and hesitated as my hand wrapped around the doorknob.

"No time to second guess yourself, Eden. Just get out there and do what needs to be done." The pep talk did little to motivate me, but I pushed ahead regardless.

The hall was bustling with servants and some of the other

women participating in the Trials. Catching a glimpse of Pimea, who was dressed in a silken gown that was the color of blue skies, she beckoned me. I figured I may as well speak with her, seeing as how I wouldn't have another opportunity to do so after that night.

"Eden, you look amazing." She gawked and twirled her finger, pointing at the floor. I grinned and obliged. With a spin, the glittering gems caught every ounce of light from the torches lining the halls, which were burning with regular fire that night. The skirt caught the movement and floated around me like a feather.

"Wow, your seamstress is an artist. Can I borrow her?" She asked with a scrunched nose while holding up the skirt on her gown.

"I think you look exquisite," I replied. It wasn't a lie either. She didn't even need makeup to look gorgeous, and her toned body looked fantastic underneath the silk, which showed every curve that she possessed. Pimea flashed me a dazzling smile before being pulled on by one of her servants that very much resembled my own.

"I suppose it is time for me to be going. I will see you there."

"See you," I smiled back sadly.

As soon as she had gone, I drew the map from my cleavage, where I had hidden it. Trying to make sense of the map wasn't as easy as I had thought it would be. I could tell which room was mine because it had a Celtic knot on top of it, all I had to do was count how many of the doors were not mine before the next hallway. Easy-peasy, right?

I turned the opposite way of where I was used to traveling when leaving my room. With a glance backward, I saw a flash of Scott's shiny black hair bobbing through the crowds. Shit. I started outright running. The further I got down the hall, the more the crowd started to disperse. I nearly toppled over as I rammed straight into one of the tiny servant women.

"Watch it!" She sneered angrily.

"I'm so sorry," I said without stopping. I could feel her large gray eyes on my back. Turning down the next hall, and then the next, until I had eventually come to a part of the castle that was entirely different from what I was accustomed to. The atmosphere there was darker, more dangerous. It sent goosebumps over my flesh. I looked over the map again, concluding that I was a mere few turns from Rowan's room.

The flames flickering along the walls were darker, somehow, and they burned with an eerie glow that nearly matched the crimson of my hair. Had this been a movie, I would have been the one in the audience screaming at myself to turn and run away. If horror movies had taught me anything, it was that you don't walk down creepy dark hallways when you are alone. With my heart pounding in my chest, I listened carefully for the sound of footsteps. Satisfied that I couldn't hear any, I pressed forward, completing the last stretch of my journey.

I swallowed against the dry lump in my throat upon approaching Rowan's bedroom door. It was easily twice the size of the door that led to my own and was an oily black color. Laying a hand upon it, it felt cold and uninviting. Like, walking through it might be the last thing I ever did. Footsteps and the clanking of armor from down the hall made me jump in my skin.

"It's now or never," I whispered, shoving the map back into my cleavage and pushing the door open just enough to slip through. I quickly shut it behind me, pressing myself up against it until the footsteps were just on the other side. *Fuck, fuck, fuck!* I searched the room for a closet, a chest, just anything that I could climb into, really. Deep voices rumbled from the other side, though I couldn't make out a word of what they were saying. Did they know I was there? Surely that was impossible.

Then again, I was in a magical Realm, full of magical jerks who kept surprising me. My eyes fell on the bed, it was high enough from the floor that I could easily slide under it. With a sigh, I looked down, remembering I was wearing enough fabric to dress the royal army. There was no way I was getting out of the ball gown on my own after it had taken a team to put it on me in the first place. Just as quickly as they had started, the voices went quiet.

I pressed my ear against the door and heard the footsteps resume. I released the breath I had been holding inside my lungs. Trying to remember what I was looking for, I took a step further into the room. Rowan's bed was absolutely massive, like, tiny football field kind of huge. The dark black pillowcases and blankets greatly contrasted from the reserved, good-prince look he sported. Beyond the bed was an enormous desk that was stacked with parchments and books.

At the end of the bed was a long, rectangular chest that had been adorned with fine golden symbols. I unlatched the hook and pulled it open to find an array of weapons. From axes, swords, and bows with full quivers, Rowan was prepared for anything. I shut the lid and redid the latch before making my way to the desk. It sat between a wall with built-in bookshelves that inhabited the same leather-bound book as the room Scott and I had used as a practice area.

I scanned the desk for anything that looked like it might contain the crystal I was looking for, without any luck. The only contents of the desk were papers written in languages I couldn't understand and ledgers of all kinds. Moving away from it, I gave the room another scan. My sights settled on the mantle of the fireplace. Upon it sat a shining silver case with tiny claw feet. I gave the door a glance before making my way to it and pulling open the lid.

Inside lay crystals of all shapes and colors. Amber was the one I was looking for, I remembered after a quick search through my memories. Harper had used that shade of crystal when he had opened the portal. He had also said something, though I couldn't remember the word. Resting my eyes on a crystal that met the color I was looking for, I pulled it from the case and returned to the desk. The papers made a beautiful crackling noise, one that only parchment could give, as I sifted through them, trying to find anything that might help. No such luck.

Books, those are a good source of information.

I began to sift through the various titles. Some of them didn't even *have* titles, while most were in foreign languages. My heart leaped in my chest as I finally found one with the words "Human Realm." written in bold down the spine. Flipping through the pages, I searched for anything to do with a portal. Halfway through the text, I heard a noise from across the room that sent the book falling from my fingers and clattering against the floor.

"Hello?" I croaked. My throat grew tight as I noticed two glowing green eyes watching me from the far corner on the other side of the bed. The eyes grew brighter as the owner stood, moving closer to the bed. I could just make out a mass of black, silky curls in the dimly lit room.

"Is it normal, where you are from, to go through other people's things after breaking into their bedrooms?" Rowan's voice was low and husky. It made me feel like a fly that had wandered into the web of a spider. Well, the spider was home, and I was stuck in its trap. I couldn't force my words to come out, and just stood there gawking like an idiot as he made his way around the bed.

His stride was purely animalistic like he really was hunting me now. I didn't move a muscle as he bent down beside me to retrieve the book.

"Human Realm? Planning an escape, are we?"

Everything inside was screaming at me to abort the mission, get the hell out of there, and run for the hills. But my traitorous body was frozen in place. Not just from fear, I actually couldn't force myself to move. Trying to step forward, it felt like an invisible chain had been looped around my ankles. Struggling against the unseen force, I winced as Rowan took another step in my direction.

"You're not the only one that holds power, little Witch. Now tell me," His breath was white-hot against my flesh when he leaned into an eye-level position. I couldn't fight it, not even to turn my head away. When he spoke, his voice had dropped even lower, the tone made me shiver down to the bone. "What did you think you could accomplish? I have the finest warriors at my fingertips. Did you not think about what would happen, had you managed to leave?"

I felt the tightness holding my throat loosen, just enough for me to manage a few words.

"I have a feeling you're going to tell me."

His laugh was eerie as it rumbled through his chest. Something dark, and nothing like the laugh I had heard in the garden.

"Mouthy." He said with a wicked smile on his lips. He pulled his head back and straightened his shoulder, returning to his full height. Probably a scare tactic, I figured. And it was working. My legs were trembling uncontrollably beneath the massive skirt. I was aware of every sensation as he brought three fingers brushing against my collarbone. The touch was gentle enough to make my eyes flutter shut with pleasure. He continued to move his fingers against me as he circled, caressing my exposed shoulders, and the top half of my back.

"Had you managed to escape," he continued. "I would have hired the bounty hunter again. But I wouldn't have stopped there. You are smart, so you would have probably evaded him for as long as possible. So, I'd also pay good coin to the mercenaries in every tavern from here to the Demonlands. They might bring you back, but it wouldn't be in one piece."

"So, you would have me killed for going home?" I tried to glare at him but only managed to do so at the bed in front of me. His spell felt like one hundred pounds of fresh sap had been poured onto me. Everything felt like it was happening in slow motion. Even his touch felt like an echo on my flesh. But he was bluffing, I could feel it in my heart. "You already caught me trying to leave, so why not kill me yourself, right now?"

His hands shot up, snaking around my throat as he pulled his lips to my ear.

"Are you testing me, Witch? You have no idea who I am or what I've done to your kind. The things I've seen would make you scream. Make you beg for mercy."

"I don't beg. Ever." I snapped.

The remark pissed him off enough to make him jerk me around to face him. His hand moved to a position in the air between us, his fingers curled in as he summoned his power, calling it to his palm with words completely unfamiliar to me. An eruption of indigo smoke and sparks flowed from his hand. The magic lifted me up, off of the floor, and moving through the air. I settled on my back, on top of his bed. As much as I had hoped it would interrupt his other spell that bound my arms and legs, it hadn't. I watched helplessly as he climbed onto the bed, hovering his massive body above me.

His wandering eyes devoured my exposed skin, flashing brightly as he moved them across every exposed inch of my upper half.

"Lift your arms above your head, puppet." He whispered with another brutish smirk. Hating my traitorous arms as they obeyed his command, I glared at his gorgeous face. Watching as he brought his knees to either side of my hips, I wondered if Ellie would be mad about him disrespecting her dress creation this way.

"Don't mess up my gown."

"My intentions are not on the gown. Unless you are speaking of removing it, which doesn't sound like a bad idea..."

I wished at that moment that I could pull my knees together in response to the moisture building between my thighs. Rowan sat back against his heels and smoothed his hands over my arms, starting at my shoulders and moving his way up to my wrists. With his power still weighing me down, it was unnecessary for him to hold them there, but that's what he did. I watched his lips as they parted enough for him to exhale heavily.

Something deep in my gut told me to ask him for it, to beg for a kiss. I needed it so badly that I felt like I was being tortured inside. If only I could lean forward, just a few inches is all it would take to close the distance between us. He could easily hike up my skirt and give me what I was longing for if he would just...

"You hunger for me, don't you?" He growled. The words were dripping with honey, feeding the part of my soul that wanted exactly that. What was wrong with me? I hated him and had from the moment I met him. It must be some kind of Fae magic, I determined. Never in my right mind would I desire someone who kidnapped me and talked to me like I was his slave.

"Not in the least," I snapped back.

"Lie if you'd like, but I can smell your arousal. It's all over you."

"When was the last time you had your nose checked?"

"Don't want to admit it? Fine, let's test it, shall we?"

Dipping his head low, I felt his lips brush my skin. The contact brought a fresh wave of desire, stirring deep within me. An ache was beginning in my core, begging to be released. Closing my eyes tightly, I tried to push the feeling away. Rowan went even further, trailing his hand back down my arms and up to turn my head to the side. His teeth scraped against my skin, provoking a moan to escape me.

"Your body is telling you something. Care to explore it further?" His deep voice vibrated through my skin. I bit my tongue to keep from agreeing to what he was suggesting, reminding myself that it was his Fae powers making me feel this way. Did Fae even have that kind of power? I had no idea. But it made me feel a little less wrong by telling myself they did. Rowan didn't wait for an answer before bringing his teeth to my neck. He bit down gently, sending a flood of heat and wetness between my legs.

I was just about to crack wide open, to tell him to ravage my body from head to toe. Instead, he sat back with that devilish grin and moved from the bed. I opened my eyes to peer at him, hating the sinking in my chest as he waved his hand, releasing me from his hold. I swallowed hard against the dryness in my throat as I pushed myself up and moved away from his bed. Another wave of his hand had a fist pounding at the door.

"In." He called. Four guards burst through the door, swords at the ready.

Chapter Twelve

"YOU BASTARD," I CRIED AT HIM WITH WIDE EYES, TERRIFIED that I was about to be cut down by the guards for my crimes. Rowan held a hand up to them and approached me. I stared at him with a glare that could have melted that stupid smirk off of his face.

"That's no way to speak to the future king. Now," his grin widened as he pointed a finger at the floor, "kneel, and apologize."

"No fucking—"

"I said kneel, Witch." He commanded once more. With a snap of his fingers, I crumbled to my knees, my chin parallel with the floor. I thought we had moved past this whole 'controlling my body' thing. Looking up at him, I could see the enjoyment he was getting from playing with me like a puppeteer.

"Try again," he said through clenched teeth.

With a glance at the guards, who were prepared to do anything he asked of them, with their hands still on the hilt of their swords. Looking back at him, I flared my nostrils, wanting nothing more than to tear him to pieces in front of his buddies in armor. Through a clenched jaw, I reluctantly gave him what he wanted.

"I'm sorry for going through your stuff," I growled.

"See? That wasn't too painful."

I felt my body go heavy, once again under my control. Rowan offered me a hand, which I accepted, only so he wouldn't have another reason to do his little magic trick again. Once I was firmly on my feet, he motioned to the guards.

"Wait outside, she will need to be escorted to the ball."

Like good little dogs, they left the room in a hurry. Rowan's gaze settled on me once the door had been shut. Holding an open hand toward me, I looked back at him with drawn eyebrows.

"The crystal," he ordered. I had all but forgotten that it was still clamped in my fist. Uncurling my fingers, I gingerly held it out to him without a word. He plucked it from my palm and walked to the tiny box I had retrieved it from, placing it back where it belonged. Well, there went my last chance of getting out of this mess and returning to my family. I could feel the tears stinging my eyes but refused to let them fall down my cheeks.

"Now, shall we?" He sighed and returned to the professional-prince attitude he carried during the greeting in the grand hall. He held an arm out in a gesture for me to lead the way through the door. I tore my eyes away from him and obliged, did what he wanted me to, shoulders slumped in defeat.

The guards stood in the hall, patiently waiting for us. Silence settled in as we began the trek to the ballroom as a group. It felt like I was doing some fucked-up walk-of-shame for the entirety of the walk. I'd be lying if I said that I didn't want to turn around and head back to Rowan's bedroom to finish what he had started. Perhaps if I told him how much I wanted him all over me, he would give me what my body was craving.

I shook the thought from my mind as we approached the ballroom. The heavy double doors had been propped open, revealing a beautifully decorated room that was big enough to occupy a small city. Massive chandeliers, that were easily as big as my house, hung in three rows. They were dripping with gems and glittered like diamonds against the candles burning in them. Beneath the light fixtures lay a glossy, onyx floor that reflected the lights in flickers as people swept across it.

A group of musicians played string instruments to a perfect tempo for a couple's dance. Rowan stepped to my side. I looked around him, noticing that the guards had disappeared. He looked at me with a gentleman's smile, making my knees wobble. Holding a hand out for me, he lifted a brow.

"Care to dance?" he asked quietly.

After what had just transpired, I wasn't sure if he was asking or telling me, so I accepted the invitation, letting him lead me to the center of the floor. Eyes of envy settled on us as he placed one hand on the small of my back while still holding the other lightly in his own. It was making it really hard to keep hating him, with him acting like less of a controlling dick.

"Lord Blaive," I whispered with a grimace on my face. "I-- uh...I don't know how to dance."

He grinned at me, and for a second, I thought I saw a glimmer of kindness in those gorgeous eyes of his.

"Would you like for me to make you dance?"

"No," I snapped, looking around at the hundreds of pairs of eyes watching us. "I just thought you should be aware that I'm about to make a fool out of us."

"Speak for yourself," He chuckled and began to pull me in strides across the dance floor. I felt like he was taking it easy on me, as I found it easy to follow his steps while we danced. Twirling me with one hand I let a laugh slip out of me, which made him smile. It felt almost comfortable with him leading. I was sure that I would look like a headless chicken without him to guide me.

"You seem to be enjoying yourself," He grinned and pulled me close, after twirling me around, causing my skirt to billow around both of our legs. I allowed him to press my palm against his hard chest. My eyes followed the movement before traveling to meet his dazzling gaze.

"It's not the worst thing I've ever done."

I don't know how long we had been dancing, nor how many songs the band had played since the start, but I knew I felt content in Rowan's arms, like I was floating and he alone kept me grounded. A flash of his lips pressed against mine played through my head as he smiled, my heart fluttered with each step. Every time his skin brushed against mine as we swayed, I thought about being in his room, and him on top of me. My body craved more.

Rowan lowered me into a dip. I let my head fall back, extending my neck so that it was fully exposed to him. His lips brushed against it, like they had in the bedroom. The touch sent a fizzle of electricity through my veins. To my disappointment, it was cut short when he pulled me back up to finish the dance as the music died out. Applause erupted around us, and I wasn't sure if it was meant for Rowan and me or the band. We bowed to each other formally.

"Ava would have loved this place," I said, finishing the bow and standing upright. Rowan clasped my hand in his own. I looked down at our fingers as they entwined.

A sinking feeling in my gut cut through my joy. With a sharp jab that went straight up into my heart, I knew shouldn't be having fun. Certainly not with the man standing in front of me. My father was at home dying, if not dead by now, while I left my sister to take care of him by herself. The smile faded from my lips, and I took my hand from Rowan's to pull away. He tilted his head slightly to one side, a look of confusion was tight on his brow.

"Something wrong?" His voice almost sounded genuinely concerned. I shook my head and stared at my reflection in the glassy dance floor. I was a fraud, a pretender that had been dolled up and made to look like a princess while my family suffered. Perhaps I should have let Ava come in my place. Dealing with this bullshit might have been easier on her than getting abandoned by her older sister and left with a father who had all but run out of time.

"No, I'm fine." I lied and turned to leave. Rowan's hand caught my elbow. Much to my surprise, this time, it was gentle, unlike the normal demanding touches I was used to when concerning him.

"You aren't fine. You mentioned your sister, Avangeline, correct?"

"I said I'm fine," I muttered and pulled my arm out of his hold. Rowan's eyes glistened in the flickering candlelight as he allowed me to do so. I could feel him watching me as I scurried from the ballroom. Pimea tried to get my attention from several feet away, but I pretended I couldn't hear. The world was changing. I felt like I was becoming another person and couldn't stop it. This realm was messing with my mind. I could hear footsteps following me as I walked back through the double doors we had come in.

Trying to remember how to get back to my room, I started walking as fast as I could. My heart raced at the sound of the feet behind me. He knew something was wrong, though I wasn't sure why he cared. Rowan didn't seem to care about much of anything when it came to my life. To him, I was just a 'filthy Witch.' I turned down a hall that I wasn't entirely sure I should have and picked up the pace of my feet. The footsteps grew louder behind me, and I started to turn, to tell him to fuck off...

"I told you I'm fine, you don't need to--Scott?"

"Hey there. Wow...you look lovely tonight, Eden." Scott said with a smile. "Now, what's going on? I saw you leave the prince on the dancefloor and thought you might be troubled about something, judging by the way you practically ran from the room."

I took a moment to look at Scott, in his formal attire that matched his gleaming black ponytail. He looked handsome, with his piercing blue eyes, and a touch of stubble growing along his chin.

"Thanks, Scott, you look good as well." I turned and started to make my way back to my room again. Scott followed at my side, his ears wide open for me. "I'm fine, really, I was just thinking of how much I miss Ava and dad, that's all."

"The look on your face says that isn't the only thing on your mind." I glanced at the hard line forming between his brows. "Is it Rowan again? Did he hurt you?"

"No!" I said with a laugh that came off sounding like something that would come out of a donkey. Jesus. Now he was for sure going to know that something was up. The truth was, I was also thinking about my encounter with Rowan. How much I had wanted him, how intoxicated I felt when he kissed my neck...

"Eden, you need to tell me if something is going on," Scott grabbed my shoulder and whipped me around to face him. I rolled my eyes when he held my hands softly between his and looked at me with those intense eyes. "I can protect you."

"What are you gonna do if I say yes, storm the castle with me? Start a very short battle to our deaths?" I snorted and spun around.

"I would never allow something like that to happen to you, Eden. But the Coven has its ways of protecting our own. We could remove you from this place, hide you, and place you under the protection of our strongest spellcasters. Say the word, and I can make that happen for you."

"And then they would find my sister and my father. They would kill them, Scott."

He rubbed the stubble on his chin and sighed, keeping his eyes on me the entire time. I started to walk and immediately remembered that I had no clue where the hell I was going. Grinding my teeth, I looked at him again.

"Look, I'm sorry. I know that you are just trying to help. I can handle myself when it comes to Rowan," I placed a hand on his shoulder. "What I *do* need help with is finding my way back to the room, please."

Scott chuckled and nodded in resignation as he pointed to the left.

"This way, princess," he said softly, taking my arm in his, just like he had the first day we met. It seemed like so long ago, despite being only a few days. Harper had told me that time moves differently here, and I thought that I was beginning to understand what he meant by that. Walking with Scott was like a breath of fresh air. He was handsome, but not like Rowan. No, Rowan was all man from his beautiful dark locks down to his hunting boots.

Scott was more of a pretty boy who had big puppy dog eyes and a love for the color black. I couldn't explain why, but I cared for him like he was an old friend.

"Hey, Scott, can I ask you something?"

"Of course!" He flashed me a smile.

"You said that I've been here before. Do we," I wagged a finger between the two of us. "Know each other, I mean, from back then?"

"Yes," He said slowly. "I met you when you were just a little one. Being five years older than you, I wasn't very interested in making friends with a baby. But Tamora was close with my mother, so we spent a few years together."

"A few years? How do I not remember any of that?"

"It could be a spell that was placed on you, or it could just be that you were too young to hold any memories from that time."

"Who is he?"

Scott stopped us in front of my bedroom door. I beckoned him to come in, preparing myself for the answers to the questions I was asking. I wasn't even sure if I wanted them. Dropping onto my bed sideways, due to the skirt being too large for me to sit normally, I slapped the area beside me. He closed the door quietly and made his way over to the bed, sitting down beside me.

"Who are we talking about, exactly?" he asked, searching my eyes.

"My real father."

"Eden," Scott sighed and rubbed his forehead like a strong headache was coming on. "That is something I cannot answer for you. Even if I wanted to tell you, I couldn't. Your mother went to great lengths to protect you, even from me."

"So, you don't know?" I asked with a frown.

"No. I was never told. What I *can* tell you is that your biological father was not of the Human Realm. Your mother took you there to escape from something or *someone*. And when she did, my mother and many others who cared for Tamora protected her place on the throne. We knew, when the time came, she would be ready to return and aid the Coven."

The memory of my mother walking through the living room door passed through my mind.

"Aid the Coven in what, exactly?"

"It's really not my place to say, Eden."

"Whose place is it to say then? What was she running from? Is there anything that you can tell me?" I could feel heat filtering through my veins. Scott took notice and scooted away to the foot of the bed. His eyes were wide with the knowledge that I had powers that I couldn't yet control. It didn't help that every time I grew angry, my powers swelled inside of me.

"Please calm yourself. I'm here to help you. Not to piss you off. The Coven's council controls the information of its members. A good place to start would be there. Or..."

"Or what?" I practically shouted, feeling the burn itching under my skin, begging to be released.

"Lord Blaive. His kingdom is the highest on the food chain, meaning any information that happens in the smaller kingdom goes through here as well."

Pondering this, I wasn't sure if I wanted to discuss something so intimate with the prince. It was one thing to want to bed someone, and a whole other thing to want to discuss all of the details of your troubled past. Yet, if I decided not to, I might

THREE DEADLY TRIALS

never learn anything about my mother or myself. It was a need that had burned inside of me since I watched her walk through that door, figuring she was just running off into the sunset to forget about us. The boiling in my veins calmed to a simmer and then stopped completely.

"I'll talk to him."

"I'll come with you."

"No," I shook my head and began picking at my nails. "I think it's something that I should do on my own. No offense to you, of course."

"I understand." He nodded.

"Another question?"

"Go ahead."

"Was my mother a good person? I mean, the beings around here talk about Witches like we are horrible, evil even. My mother was the queen of our Coven. Did she do something bad? Did she hurt people?"

Scott's eyes filled with sadness, and he moved closer, taking my hand in his. This time it didn't feel as awkward. It felt like someone who truly loved me, and had loved my mother, seeking to comfort me. I gazed into those deep, azure eyes and waited for him to respond.

"Your mother was the best there has ever been, Eden. She was kind, loving, and compassionate. When she--" His frown was deep, making him look on the verge of tears as he choked out the rest. "When she died, it wasn't because of anything that she had done wrong. Evil didn't turn your mother's heart black. She was a healer, a pure soul. I can assure you of that."

The tears in my eyes spilled over at his words. Maybe it was the emotions of knowing my mother wasn't the monster I had made her out to be, or maybe it was that Scott had been the one to deliver the enlightening information. Whatever it was, I had no reason to do what I did next, which was to sit up, cup Scott's face in my hands and press my lips against his.

I closed my eyes as I felt the bed shake as he leaned into the kiss, the smell of fire and ash filled my nose. His hand made its way up my back and entangled in my mass of curls. Green, glowing eyes flashed behind my eyelids. The feeling of Rowan's body pressed against mine, the spicy smell on his skin, his touch that was firm and demanding. My eyes popped open, and I jerked away from Scott, pressing my fingers to my lips, regretting what I had done in an instant.

"Eden..."

"I'm so sorry," I said and scrambled away from the bed, my fingers still firmly against my mouth. "You should go."

"Can we talk about what just happened?"

"No," I said with wide eyes as I looked at him and swung open the door. "I'm sorry. Please, go."

Scott looked hurt and I didn't blame him. How could I have done something so stupid? With slumped shoulders, Scott rose from the bed and left through the door. When he passed by me, I could see that he wanted to speak, to say anything that could save this moment for him. I didn't give him the chance and hurried in, slamming the door on his dumbfounded face.

I stood there, feeling like an idiot until a knock on the door made me jump. Staring at it, I knew that I should open it and apologize again, tell him that I hadn't meant it. That it had been a mistake. Making up my mind that it would be the right thing to do, I flung the door open. My mouth closed as I realized that the face on the other side, was not the one I had been expecting.

"Hello, mistress, I heard that you had left the event. I've come to get you out of that dress. Unless you'd like to sleep in it?" She snorted, amused at her joke. I noticed a wheelbarrow beside her and figured she had brought it to help her in transporting the gown.

"No, no. Please," I motioned her in and stood in silence as she undid the beautiful dress. As soon as it hit the floor, I felt like I had just lost fifty pounds. She proceeded to leave after she removed my corset, and I had helped her in loading the massive dress into her little wheelbarrow. Pulling a sleep gown over my head, I shoved my arms into it and crawled into bed to reflect on the events of that evening.

Well, all of them except what I had done with Scott. I shoved the thought of that as far from my mind as I possibly could. Instead, I focused on Rowan. There was something about that sexy smile, the way he took control...

I had grown wet for him, desiring to see what lay beneath his clothes. I ached to feel his erection thrust up against me, required it inside of me. My stomach exploded with butterflies, as though I could feel him watching with me as the images ran through my mind. I forced the smutty thoughts aside with a dissatisfied grunt. Slumber embraced me immediately that evening. I dreamt of Rowan and all the things I could do to serve him... if only he were mine.

Chapter Thirteen

I AWOKE THE NEXT MORNING TO THE SENSATION COMING FROM Ellie's small hands as they shook me. With stinging eyes, I sat up to the robust fragrance of coffee floating around the room. That made me smile at Ellie like she had been an angel, appearing to let me through the pearly gates. She seemed pleased with herself, which was nice to see. Particularly because I wasn't the one who paid her.

"Pleasant morning, miss. Your teacher, mister Ommin, is here to collect you for training. Oh, why am I standing around chatting your head off? You must be so nervous for tonight! Forgive me, mistress."

"Nervous?" I repeated in my sleepy haze.

"For the first of the Devotion Trials?" She said it like a question, unsure if I knew what she was talking about. I didn't. Nobody had thought to mention it to me. Swinging the blanket off of my legs, I slid from the bed and was immediately offered a cup of steaming coffee. I accepted it from her, sipping it carefully while Ellie laid out an outfit for me and bowed, allowing Scott to enter as she left.

I watched him approach, my mind nowhere near what had

happened between us the night before. He appeared taken aback when his eyes landed on my face, which I'm sure was red with anger, as it scrunched into a scowl.

"Wake up on the wrong side of the bed, did we?"

"Why didn't you inform me that the first Trial was going to be tonight?" I hissed through my teeth. Scott launched his hands up, and his mouth gaped like a fish out of water.

"I was going to tell you, it's just–"

"Just what, Scott? It wasn't important enough to mention to the person who will be going through with it?"

"You keep running away from me. I'm beginning to think that is all you can do." His voice was raised an octave as he squeaked the words.

It was my turn to let my mouth droop open. Moving off of the bed, I was fully prepared square up to him, despite his size. My body had other plans and by the first step I tripped over my own feet, sending scalding coffee onto my nightdress. Cursing, I slammed the cup onto the table and looked for anything I could use to get the liquid off of me. Scott came to my rescue with the bowl and cloth from the vanity, it was fresh, as it was every morning and evening when Ellie slipped in to change it out.

"What can I say? I must get it from my mother." The muttered words slipped out before I could stop them. Scott kept still in place and stared down at me as I violently rubbed myself with the rag. Breathing a heavy puff of air, I straightened, tossing the cloth back into the bowl.

"I'll wait outside while you get dressed. Keep in mind to be cautious with these garments, the Fae Royals like for their victims to look their best for the Trials."

With that, he fled the room. As soon as he had gone, my shoulders sank with a pang of guilt that twisted in my belly. I managed to finish off what was left of my coffee before dressing. Upon examination, I realized that the outfit looked almost the same as the one I had worn for my previous lessons with Scott.

Running my fingers down it, I noted that the materials were thicker, sturdier as if the garb had been built for traveling. The golden-thread embellishments were still present but shaped into tiny Celtic knots along the deep neckline. I smoothed a thumb across them, observing the cool, thick metal thread. It was lovely.

Eliminating my sleepwear, I tugged on the emerald-colored tunic along with the pants that resembled seaweed, and a new pair of boots that shone like they had been polished but never worn. I left my hair as it was for no reason other than the fact that, somehow, it had managed to stay looking the way Ellie had done it the night before. The whole look made me feel much more badass than I believed.

On the other side of the door, Scott was waiting, just like he had said he would be. We walked to the training room without a sound. I wanted to apologize but couldn't form the words on my tongue to force them out. He walked in strides, not minding that I had to jog to keep up. Anger was thick in his blood, I could feel it seeping from him and into me.

Merely in identifying his anger, heat began to saturate my insides as well. What right did he have to be mad at me? Tamora was my mother, and I had every right to be angry with her, despite him stating she'd done it all to protect me. What right did he have to love my mother more than I? To protect her against her own daughter?

A crackle of electricity shot through me, immersing the room with a tint of sapphire. *Well, that one is new*, I thought. Before I knew what I was doing, I lunged to yank back on Scott's shoulder. He stumbled mid-step and gawked at me in confusion. With one glimpse, he had dropped into a fighting stance. His fists became parallel to the floor as he held them out toward me in a way that screamed power. I observed the frost forming in his palms.

"Enough, Eden, you must try to relax. We don't have a protection spell in place, and I don't want to hurt you." His voice was solid, firm in a way I had never heard him speak before. He was afraid of me. A stab of panic shot through my stomach. Gazing down at my colored hands I regarded the energy-burning around them, snapping and crackling like it had the night Harper had collected me. It reminded me of why I was here, who I had left behind. It enraged me.

Fixing my hands in the air to imitate his, I drew one back. His azure eyes grew even wider as they followed me in bringing it forth, slamming my fist onto the floor. I watched in slow motion as his body lifted from the ground due to the impact of my spell. His body tumbled through the air while instant regret chilled my bones. I wrung my hands, trying to make the bolts of electricity disappear back into my fingers while Scott slammed into a book-shelf. Books tumbled down around him as well as pages that had been ripped from them by force.

"Scott, I'm so sorry. I don't know what came over--" I paused as I watched him rise from the smoking heap of books. His eyes were blazing cyan, gleaming like Rowan's had the night before. Taking a step back, I held up my hands in submission as I saw his fists, clenched into tight fists, while he strode to me.

"Get your fucking hands up." He bellowed in a furious tone. Shaking my head, I disobeyed my mind and did as he had ordered. With a look on his face that said he was ready to kill, I knew that I should do anything he asked at that moment. "You want to fight? I'm going to show you how."

"No, Scott, I didn't mean it--"

I dodged to the left as he hurled a shard of spiked ice directly at my head. Great, I had forced him to go bonkers. And now he wanted to kill me. *Good job, Eden.* My thoughts were interrupted as he pulled his hand through the air, bringing it eye level with me. I only just had time to drop to the floor on my stomach, avoiding the next shard as it whizzed toward me. I looked back to watch as it smashed into pieces against the stone wall.

"Get up and fight back." He shouted.

My knees wobbled as I forced myself to my feet and brought

my hands into fists between us, trying to summon the anger inside. I envisioned myself at eleven, and the image of my mother stepping away and coming to this place. She left us, her family, to maintain her stupid Coven. My insides began to twist as I watched Scott prepare another attack. A single lock of hair began to swirl against my cheek, whipping against my fair skin as I felt the dam breaking in me, freeing my powers.

Instinct took over my body amidst Scott's next attack. With one swift movement, I sliced my hand through the air and watched his ice splinter, fracturing down the middle as it flew toward me. With another sweep of my hand, the two halves split apart and pushed aside, both of them whizzing past my ears.

The blue haze was more intense than ever as my eyes locked onto Scott. My fingers seemed to have a mind of their own as they began to wind through the air. A breeze elevated the curls from my shoulders. The faster I moved my hands, the more intense the gusts became. I didn't stop until the pressure was roaring in my eardrums, and I could feel my hair lashing against my face, leaving it stinging. The floor fell out from under me as I relaxed into the element surrounding me.

Closing my eyes, I leaned into the storm. Scott's shouts were barely audible over the raging whirlwind around me. I reopened my sights to locate my target. Scott's face had gone calmer, his eyes were staring directly into mine as I opened my arms like wings. My heart thundered inside of me as I slammed my palms together, sending the force of my spell into Scott. It hit him like a sledgehammer to the chest.

My feet slammed back to the ground as the rustling of pages calmed and all I could hear was the sound of Scott panting. He was on his ass, staring at me in disbelief as his chest heaved. Releasing the power, I felt its influence leave me.

"Very...good," he managed between gasps.

"You okay?" I asked, lending him a hand. He allowed me to

help him up. While dusting off his pants I couldn't help but notice the shit-eating grin on his face. Pride, I could sense it.

"I'm fine. Or I will be, once I walk off the beating I just took."

"You asked for it, remember?" I smiled.

"I did, but I've never seen anything like that. I'm willing to bet, with the right training, you can elevate your power even further. But that...what you just did, it was something incredible."

"What do you mean? It's just another power. You can shoot freaking icicles out of your hands!"

"You don't even realize what you've done," He said in awe, a smile on his lips.

With the way he was watching me now, I wasn't sure I wanted to know.

Chapter Fourteen

"Eden, you fed off of my emotions and manifested them into yourself. Empaths are unheard of in our world anymore, but it sounds like you may be one."

I shrugged, smoothing my hands over my hair, which was filled with static. Scott shook his head and lifted his eyebrows at me, expecting some sort of response.

"Cut me some slack, Scott, I didn't even know I had any powers at all a week ago. Forgive me for not being as excited as you *clearly* are. Can we talk about something else, like, why you were mad at me earlier?" Scott didn't say anything, leaving it open for me.

"Look, I'm sorry for what I said. I'm sorry for what I felt. Forgive me?"

He sighed and looked at the table to his far left.

"Help me get our lessons for the day picked up and organized, then I will forgive you."

With a glance at the disordered table, I groaned but nodded in agreement. We began to clean the tipped bottles and, thankfully, they appeared to have remained intact for the most part. Scott started naming off ingredients that sounded like they had come from a storybook. The list went on and on, over hundreds of tiny bottles, each containing odd bits and pieces of things.

"Today we will be focusing on two very different potions. You will be in the wilds, which can be dangerous."

"The wilds, like, the enchanted forest outside of the castle?" I asked with a horrified stare.

"I'm sorry, Eden, I can't tell you anything more about your location for tonight or what you will be doing there. The best I can do is show you how to protect yourself with alchemy. You will be able to bring two potions with you. I'm going to teach you to make one for illumination and another for clairvoyance."

"How long will the Trial last?" I asked as he set up a mortar and pestle along with various bottles of ingredients.

"As long as it takes you to figure it out." He said simply and started to pour things into the bowl. "Illumination requires very little, it's a fairly simple potion. You will need a touch of Silver Mist, two ounces of Sap of Enchanted Tree, a drop of Water of the Hidden Spring, and twelve crushed diamonds."

"Simple," I muttered under my breath with an eye-roll for good measure. Observing as he mixed the ingredients, I noticed the smell of fresh rain as he poured them into an empty bottle. After corking the bottle filled with a light blue liquid, he handed it off to me.

"When you need some light, pour this potion onto a thick, fallen branch. Make sure it is one that you can take with you as it is a one-use potion."

"Got it," I said and shoved the bottle into my pocket. "Next?"

"Next is clairvoyance. This potion is to be consumed and will allow your mind to think in ways that it wouldn't normally. Technically, this potion can be so potent as to show you the future. However, Blaive's council deemed it too strong and a potential cheat, so I had to dull it down enough so that it works like a brain booster."

"So, I won't be seeing my future tonight?" I feigned a pout.

Scott laughed and cleaned the bowl before beginning to pour the ingredients for the second potion into it.

"No, you won't become a seer, not tonight anyway. Now, this potion is a bit more complicated, even the simplified version. For this one, you will need precisely four teaspoons of gold dust, three Dragon Leaves, a pinch of Trollie Buds, a fistful of crushed Leaves of the Clover, and a slosh of Liquified Ashes."

"Sounds ridiculous," I spoke aloud, baring my teeth in regret as Scott shot me a glare.

"As absurd as it sounds, these are centuries of recipes that have been passed down after years and decades of trial and error. Consider your ancestors and praise them for it."

"Right, sorry."

He moved onto mixing and dumping the newly-formed potion into another bottle. I took the silvery liquid from him and stuck the bottle in the same pocket as the other. Assisting in the cleanup, I tried to remember all the steps that he had taught me. Surely if these were the two things that he selected for me to bring, they had to be important, and I didn't want to be stuck in a situation without them.

"That concludes the lessons for today," Scott said, wiping his hands clean and tossing the dirty rag onto the table. "We have been here for hours, and it's nearing nightfall, which means it's almost time for you to take your place in front of the throne for the first Trial. I'll be able to accompany you inside of the throne room, but once you are moved, you are on your own."

"Scott?" I gulped against the lump rising in my throat. I didn't like the sound of being 'moved.'

"Yes?"

"I'm scared," I said with more meaning than anything I had said in my life. It showed on my face, plain as day. I could see it reflecting in Scott's tender gaze.

"You will be fine, alright? You may be at a slight disadvantage, having not grown up in our realm like the other competitors, but you are smart and strong. You can do this. I will not allow you to lose your place in the Coven, and neither will any of the others on your council."

I nodded, blinking back the hot tears in my eyes. With terror roaring in my veins, I followed Scott from the room and to our final stop for the day, which was the Throne room. Even with knots in my stomach, I was still taken by the beauty of the enormous room. The first three-quarters of the room resembled the rest of the castle, built with immaculate masonry. Beneath my feet was a five-foot-wide midnight blue carpet that stretched from the doors to the other side of the room, resting at the base of three stone steps.

Two thrones perched atop the platform the steps led to. They stood glistening with gold arms and dark blue velvet cushions. Rowan, tall and proud, stood beside them, his hands folded in front of him as he waited for me to take my place alongside the other women. All of them were dressed in clothing that mimicked my own.

Nija scoffed something under her breath as I stepped beside her, not that I cared. I was far too nervous to play her mind games.

"Welcome," Rowan commenced, just as soon as my feet had fallen into place. His voice was robust and loud like it had been at the Greeting. "I hope that all of your training has been sufficient as we enter the beginning of the Devotion Trials."

He was speaking as though he were trying to impress someone. I spared another look around the room, not able to shake the feeling that we were being watched. Four women sat in each corner, their faces covered by crisp white hoods. In front of them hovered crystal balls that were emitting surges of light. Rowan cleared his throat before continuing.

"Tonight, our competitors will perform in the Trial of Heart, in which each participant must use the morality inside of themselves to accomplish their goal. This Trial exists to prove an individual worthy of ruling a kingdom alongside her king. But it is more than that, the women must be wise in their task, for a Queen must be kind, and she must also know when it is wise to follow her head over her heart. Love, honor, and protection will see you through. May the Gods be with each of you and remember: There are no rules in these Trials, besides that, you may not kill one another."

I gave Scott a nervous glance, feeling my palms dampen with sweat as Rowan began to nod at the women in the corners of the room. Everyone besides us seven, and the four magical crystal ball users, was made to exit the room, including the prince. Just as soon as the doors closed behind us, I was hit with a wave of magic that nearly knocked me on my ass. I struggled to steady myself as another wave slammed into me.

"Pathetic," Nija laughed, holding her ground firmly.

I watched as her face began to spin, or was it my face that was spinning? I turned my head and saw that the entire room was starting to shift. The high windows that sat along the walls shattered, and from the shards trees began to grow at an alarming rate. The midnight blue carpet sprouted twigs and underbrush while the walls ballooned and crumbled open. Stumbling backward, I shoved my hands over my ears to protect them from the cracking stone that thundered in each direction.

I squeezed my eyes shut and waited for the world to stop shaking before I opened them again. When I did, the others understood it was over as well. We spared each other a look before most of them retreated into the woods that now surrounded us. Pimea looked apologetic as she, too, took off in a sprint. Not knowing what else to do, I picked a direction to start running, letting my feet carry me as fast as they could manage.

The woods were dark, making it nearly impossible to see where the hell I was going. The chiming of the two glass bottles reached my ears, reminding me that I had a potion to aid me in this. Falling to my hands and knees, I began to feel through the brush for a fallen branch. My hand wrapped around one that was just the right size, I stood and pulled it up with me. A scream ripped through my throat as I realized that what I held wasn't a branch, but the severed leg of some type of deer.

Gagging, I threw the still-warm leg as far as I could as prickles on the back of my neck settled in. An odd sound was coming from just beyond my line of sight, like a gust of wind that would pick up and then stop suddenly. I tried to follow the sound, but it ceased, making me freeze in place.

"Dangerous, aren't they? The woods, I mean." The voice was familiar. Straining my eyes, I could just make out the silhouette of a woman before she dissolved into the darkness. A hand grabbed my shoulder, but instead of ripping me to pieces like I thought it would, the grip loosened and vanished. The sound of laughter erupted behind me, like nails on a chalkboard. I knew that laugh.

"Lavinia?" I called softly.

Sure enough, the Vampire stepped in front of me with a whooshing noise, her eyes glowing like a wild animal. Scarlet blood, fresh, dripped from her chin just below a wicked smile that exposed her razor-sharp fangs.

Chapter Fifteen

"FRIGHTENED, LITTLE WITCH?" SHE LEANED IN. THE COPPERY smell of blood flooded into my senses, making it even harder not to throw up. Shaking in my boots scared, I knew she could see it, hear it, smell it on me. "Don't be afraid, not of me anyway. Nija has already claimed the right to best you."

Another set of feet sounded from behind. They weren't tactless either, they were steps of a skilled navigator. Lavinia's eye gleamed even brighter as she looked past my shoulder, seeing something that I couldn't. She looked like a baby about to be handed a lollipop.

"Looks like there is another little pawn to play with if you'll excuse me."

My hair toppled back and over my shoulders as Lavinia used her superhuman speed to push beyond me. I didn't stay there to find out what she was talking about. Seeing an actual branch in a rare beam of moonlight, I picked it up and dug into my pocket for the bottle with the blue liquid inside. Once I had located it, I drew the cork from it with my teeth and dumped it onto the branch with a glance behind me. There was nobody following my tracks, at least not for now.

A burst of blinding light radiated from the wood, making it so that the forest was no longer dark. At least, not within a twenty-foot radius of me. We must have been deep in the forest, as not even the glowing mushrooms grew around the trees as they had near the keep. I ran through the dense forest, hard and as fast as my feet could carry me. My body was slick with sweat by the time I could make out a faint flicker of light ahead. It looked to be a torch. Trying to recall what little information Rowan had given, I made my way to the light.

A small clearing, just big enough to house a tiny cottage, lay in the middle of the trees. I made my way over the fallen branches and into the clearing. A twig snapped to my right, and I looked over to find Pimea and Shael making their way to the cottage as well. After seeing Lavinia, I was slightly shaken up and on edge. But I gave Pimea a wave, nonetheless.

"Approach!" Yapped a crackling voice from in front of the cottage. All three of us stood in place, attempting to locate the owner. It didn't take long. The porch contained a twisted little wooden chair that held a wrinkly old man. He hunched forward, pulling in long drags from a wooden pipe that was puffing out smoke that stank of herbs. Peering at the other two women, who shrugged, I walked to the man and bowed.

"Hello sir, we are here for Lord Blaive's Trials. Do you have any information that could assist us?"

The man's milky eyes were halfway concealed by his shaggy gray eyebrows as he looked at me with a lopsided, gummy grin.

"Lord Blaive," He rasped, tapping a twisted finger against his balding head that was covered in liver spots. Before I could say anything else his voice changed, becoming hushed and rich.

"Have you the land and sea,
To bring forth the ingredients, three.
Yet, a word to the wise.
The ingredients you seek are tied in a knot.
And you shall not find them where there is rot.

One shall fail, be it by might.
Bring the ingredients to me,
We shall see if an image of royalty is fitting for thee."

WHEN HE HAD COMPLETED THE VERSE, HIS EYES CREASED WITH a smile as he took another long pull from his pipe. I turned to the other two with my hands up in confusion.

"What do the two of you make of it?"

Shae looked deep in thought while Pimea shrugged. I turned back to the old man.

"What are the ingredients, sir?"

The little old man just continued to smile and smoke his pipe without another word.

"It's a riddle," rung in the voice of the Elven woman. She looked at me with glinting doe eyes. The snow-white outfit she wore had been left untouched by the forest and it almost glowed even in the dim light coming from my potion and the torch above the old man. "Ingredients three, what could that mean?"

"And ingredients for what?" I thought aloud. "What kind of recipe requires three ingredients?"

A sparkle caught my eye as I stared at the ground trying to search my brain. The source of the shine was the hundreds of little Celtic knots on my tunic that Ellie had sown for the Trial. I smiled at the thought, that she had taken such care to make me feel at home. As I gazed at the tiny symbols, a thought struck me.

"Pimea," I asked, walking closer to her. "What do the three points of the Celtic knot represent?"

Pimea's eyebrows drew together in consternation. Shael stepped forward and laid a perfectly shaped nail onto my tunic, tracing one of the knots as her eyes grew even wider. Her face pulled up to look at me.

"Each point has meaning. Love, honor, and protection." She used her other hand to count them up as she said each one.

"Didn't Lord Blaive say those things before we were sent here?" I asked.

"He did," She smiled and nodded at the old man. I turned and re-approached him. He sat in the chair, still smiling, his old eyes looking at me without much consideration.

"We have your ingredients. Love, Honor, and Protection."

Following the words, I let my body stiffen, expecting a gust of magic to blow us back into the castle. It never came. Slumping my shoulders with disappointment, I turned to question the others but was cut off by a high-pitched scream coming from somewhere close by. A burning in my wrist forced my eyes to look and watch as a single point of the Faerie star branded into my skin.

A gasp from Shael made me look back at her. The same thing was happening to both her, and Pimea.

"That scream belonged to Kariye, she's been bested. We must hurry, Lady Eden." Shael said with a glance over her shoulder, as though monsters were about to breach the tree line. A fleeting thought of Lavinia and her glowing white eyes passed through my mind. They had been burning brighter than Scott's illumination potion...

With a palm slap to the forehead, I remembered I still had one that might be perfect for the occasion. I withdrew my second potion and uncorked it with my teeth before swallowing the whole thing, working hard not to gag at the rotten taste of it. The effect was instantaneous and unlike anything I had ever felt before. Ideas and thoughts raced through my mind at lightning speed.

"He didn't accept the words, what else could it be?" Pimea asked in a soft voice.

"Well," Shael said carefully. Pimea stood behind her, looking through the woods. "The three points of the knot signify whole-ness. Unity."

"Unity," I repeated. My mind was buzzing with realization. "Ingredients three. Unity. Both of you come here."

"Eden—"

"Just come here, I'm not going to hurt you. The old man wants three of us. We are the points of the knot. If we say the words, each of us taking one that will complete the knot," I looked at the old man whose smile had widened. I smiled back and motioned for the other two. "We need to unite to complete the task, just as we would have to form allies among the other kingdoms. Now, come on."

Grabbing Shael's hand in one of my own and Pimea's in the other, I began by reciting the first word.

"Love."

"Honor," Pimea said with a shaky voice.

Shael looked over her shoulder again. Her large eyes were flooding with concern. I followed her gaze to the treetops. Something was moving up there, watching us. With a gentle nudge, I urged her to continue to answer the riddle. I gave her an encouraging smile as she looked back at me. With a nod, she brought the last piece of the puzzle together.

"Protection," She whispered, the word left her lips like a melody.

We gulped in unison as the world exploded into a dazzling kaleidoscope of colors. I held tightly to the other women as we stood against the ferocious wind blasting us in the face. A roaring began in my ears just as it had at the start. I could feel the spell waver as we were pushed out of the magical tunnel and back into Rowan's castle. My shaking knees hit the floor. I wanted to cry out with relief.

"Did we do it?" I urged, glancing over at Pimea who had also not been able to keep on her feet. She nodded and pointed to the thrones, where Rowan stood. His eyes were alight with satisfaction as he made his way to us, helping Pimea and me to our feet. I notice Kariye sitting on a bench on one side of the room, being tended to by a healer. Her wounds didn't look deep but she seemed shaken up.

"Well done, all of you," Rowan said, his eyes lingering on mine for a second longer than either of the other two. Was that surprise that I saw, hiding deep inside of those pale eyes? "You have passed the first Trial; therefore, each of you will automatically be qualified for the second. You may return to your quarters. We shall celebrate tomorrow with a feast."

"Wait, that's all? We don't get a prize?" I said, mostly as a joke. Rowan turned to smile at me with his perfect set of lips. He didn't say a word as he turned again, making his way back to the throne.

"Come on," Scott said, nearly causing me to jump out of my boots.

"Jesus, Scott, could you not do that?"

I heard giggles coming from the other people in the room but ignored them as Scott wrapped his arm around my shoulders and squeezed. Feeling Rowan's stare on me, I looked back briefly, with enough time to see him burning a hole in the back of Scott's head with his eyes.

"I'm so proud of you, Eden!" Scott practically screamed it through the halls as we exited. He must have been loud enough for the entire place to hear him. I looked at him with a grin. "You completed the first Trial, and in record time!"

"Well, Pimea and Shael helped with that. Plus, the Nymph girl was bested by someone that wasn't us three. Which leaves Lavinia, Sephial or Nija."

"Indeed," Scott's eyes grew darker. "Leave it to the three who tilt toward evil to best another in the first round of the Trials."

"Oh, and Nija's got it out for me. She called dibs."

"Called what?"

"She told the others that I'm hers, to best that is. And I guess they listened to her. Lavinia was close enough to rip my throat out, but she didn't."

"The protection spells wouldn't have allowed her to 'rip your throat out.'"

"Do you have to get all teacher-y right now?" I stomped my

foot as we approached my room door. "I just freaking won the first Trial. Be happy for me."

"I am!" Scott cried with a laugh. "Now get some sleep, you've earned it. Only two more days until the second Trial. You can tell me all about it tomorrow."

"Roger that," I said with a salute before entering my room. I bathed myself from head to toe as best as I could before sliding into a comfortable sleep dress. The bed had never felt so fantastic against my skin as it did that night. I'm not even sure if my head hit the pillow before I was out like a light.

Chapter Sixteen

My lessons with Scott came to a close the next day. It was around dinner time when he realized that he had all but bored me to death by making me learn alchemy basics. He must have seen it in my eyes because, after several hours of the same thing over and over, he finally told me I was free to go and get ready for the feast. Ellie had already brought a gown for me to wear, it was lying on my bed when I returned, along with a pair of pale blue flats.

The dress was unlike anything I had ever seen before. Fabrics that mimicked chiffon, if chiffon had been crafted by the gods, subtly changed from violet to aqua depending on where the light hit them. There were no sleeves on the dress as it was held up by a piece that circled my neck, leaving my shoulders wholly exposed. In the center of the neckpiece was an enormous oval-shaped amethyst. Connecting that piece to the bottom half was a line of smaller amethyst, which were set in gold casings.

The gown hugged me around the waist and flowed loosely past my toes in a mixture of duotone patterns. Six bangles, three for each arm, were also adorned with gems, and a single piece of the multicolored cloth was linked between each arm-set. These were placed strategically by Ellie so that the fabric along my arms merged beautifully with my dress skirt.

She also set a silver circlet atop my head. The metal had been crafted with skilled hands; some of the intricate loops were no thicker than a strand of hair. Gems matching the gown had been set into the circlet so that they would catch the light even in the dimmest of settings. It would be perfect for the feast, which would be taking place in the largest of the keep's gardens, one I hadn't been to thus far, and just after sunset.

Ellie didn't pin my hair back that night but instead focused on leaving it in its natural, curly state, hanging down to my hips. She swiped a bit of onyx onto my eyelashes before sending me on my way. Scott had shown me the way earlier, as he would be too busy to escort me. I was proud of myself when I arrived, on time, and in the right place.

In utter awe, I gazed around at the setup. Heavy wooden tables had been placed on the lush grass underneath enormous white canopies. Twinkling lights that looked like a million fireflies lit up the dining area, dangling down the sides of the canopy to give the soft appearance of walls. I stepped further in, taking deep breaths of the many aromas of food that filled the air as servants began to fill the tables.

Watching as they strode by with arms full of plates, I looked at all of the different types of food they carried. Lemon and pepper salmon, cheese-covered potatoes, roast duck that had been seasoned and cooked to golden perfection, as well as hundreds of other things. An assortment of sweets lined the tables, as well as spiced wine and ale. Music was filling the air alongside the smell of food. It sounded like someone plucking the strings of a harp, which went nicely with the random chatter.

Snatching a piece of cinnamon bread off of a serving platter, I ignored the glare from the servant and walked through the hanging lights for a better look of the garden itself. What lay on the other side resembled the other gardens I had been in before.

With its enormous fountain that spat a melodic flow of water down into its base, I made my way around it and noted that there was no one else venturing like I was.

Just beyond the fountain I could see something pale on the ground at the far end of the garden. Whatever it was, it was being lit by moonlight. Deciding to investigate, I approached the break in the hedges to find a cobblestone path. With a look back, I ate my last bite of bread and started to make my way down the path.

It twisted and turned into somewhat of a maze. With no fear of getting lost, I started to turn down different corners. The moon lit the pathway enough for me to see the gems on my dress glittering in its light. I felt like a child, sneaking into my father's room while he slept to crawl into bed next to him. The thrill of it was intoxicating.

"Are you lost?" Rowan said softly from over my shoulder. My heart leaped inside of my chest as I spun on my heels to face him. A roguish grin was pulling at his lips. I gave the area a quick survey, as though I had no idea how or when I got there.

"Yeah, I think I am." I lied with pursed lips.

"How did you even get in here?"

"I, uh, well..." My mind went blank as his fresh aroma hit me right in the face. God, he smelled so good that it made me want to taste him.

"I'm impressed with you. I didn't expect that you would make it past the first Trial, and yet, you were one of the first to return." He said, changing the subject. I sighed in relief and held my ground.

"It wasn't as bad as I thought it would be," I shrugged and wagged a hand in front of me. "No big deal."

Rowan slipped his hand into mine before it had time to fall back to my side. With a gentle pull, he drew me closer, smoothing a rogue curl behind my ear as he gazed into my eyes. My breath hitched in my lungs as I saw the usual hard-ass look on his face soften.

"It *is* a big deal, Eden." He whispered, leaning closer.

"Wait," I said, leaning my head back to keep eye contact. "Did you just say my name?"

"Eden is your name, is it not?" He purred.

"Well, yeah, but you always call me 'Witch.' Why the sudden change?" I didn't trust this. Not that I didn't like the sound of my name on his tongue, I was blindsided by it.

"I like Eden better, don't you?"

I opened my mouth to agree but was interrupted by a loud boom followed by whistling coming from the direction of the castle. I bent my neck to locate the source, only to find a stream of sparks shooting into the colorful sky above us. Rowan lifted his head to watch with me as the line traveled further until it finally exploded into a shower of glittering colors.

"Fireworks," I breathed, looking back at Rowan, who was still watching the sparks of light as they disintegrated, making way for the next two fireworks that had just been shot off. My stare traveled from his eyes, which were shifting colors due to the lights in the sky, down to his perfectly kissable lips. Without allowing myself another second to think about it, I raised onto my tiptoes and pressed my mouth against his.

His eyes flashed back to view me as I closed mine and parted my lips against his. Flicking my tongue across his bottom lip, I felt his hands lower to my waist, pulling me even closer as he pushed his own tongue in between my open lips. I moaned as he retreated it so that he could nibble on my lip. Why was I enjoying it so much? I was supposed to hate this guy. He freaking kidnapped me!

I didn't care about any of that at the moment, I let his hands explore my waist and lower back as the kiss deepened. My body ached for more, and I didn't try to stop my hand as it lowered to his cock. My eyes popped open and widened at the size of him. I could feel him smile against my lips as he lifted an eyebrow at me. Well, he wasn't saying no...

"Play with mine, and I'll be forced to play with yours. Are you sure that you want that?" He growled, moving his teeth to gently bite my earlobe. I moaned again, louder this time, and let my eyes roll to the back of my head. Feeling the slick need between my legs, I panted as he started to kiss down my neck and collarbone.

Scott's words slipped into my mind, how he had said that the only people who could tell me about my mother were the Coven or the crown.

"Wait, please," I whispered, hating myself for it. "I--I want this but need to talk to you about something."

"Mmm," Rowan growled against my skin, as though it was going to take every inch of restraint that he possessed to stop kissing me. Pulling away slowly, I felt small under his gaze. His eyes were glowing, his lips rosy from the kissing. He looked at me with hardcore bedroom eyes as I took a step back and pulled free of him. I couldn't think with him so close.

"I need to ask you about my mother," I said, looking away from him. From the corner of my eye, I saw him straighten his shoulders and run a fistful of fingers through his hair.

"What would you like to know?" He asked.

"How did she die?" I let the words escape me quickly as if holding them in was damaging to my health. In a way, it was.

"She died alongside my own mother, Alara. They were deemed to be traitors to the crown."

"Deemed that by who?" My eyes shot back to his.

"My father." He replied grimly.

"Your father killed our mothers? Why?" I knew I should feel more upset about the news. But I think that deep down, I knew it would be something along these lines.

"He said they were plotting against him. Against the entire world." Rowan stood perfectly still, watching me as I absorbed the information. Rubbing my eyes, I tried to think of my next question. Before I could, Rowan continued.

"My mother was DarkFae. A Demon, to be precise. She was

forced to marry my father after winning his Devotion Trials. He assumed that she, with the aid of your mother, was feeding information to the other Demons."

"Wait. Your mother was a royal Demon? Does that mean that Nija is—"

"No," He snickered, shaking his head. "When my mother was murdered by my father, he made sure to abolish the rest of her house as well. All of them, except for me, whom he believed to be Seelie to the core. The closest set of nobility, Nija's family, rose to the throne in the Demonlands."

"Seelie?"

"A LightFae. Good through and through, until they are tainted by evil. Unseelie are what we refer to as DarkFae. They don't care about the image of goodness, or if they get caught dealing with Witches."

"Did you believe your father?" I asked quietly.

Rowan looked at me, rubbing his chin between a thumb and forefinger. Shaking his head, he lowered his hand to his side and looked around us discreetly, as though someone would behead him for speaking out about his late father.

"My father was aged and his mind had become warped during the war. I think that he became so paranoid and wary of Witches and Demons alike that he just assumed acts of treason were growing more common. Your mother was helping mine..."

"Helping her with what?" I urged in a whisper, reaching out to clutch his hand and stroke it with my fingers.

"Protecting me from my father." I could have sworn there was a glistening of tears in his eyes. I didn't have an opportunity to inquire as he turned around, tugging me back to the Garden.

"Enough chatting for one evening. Let us go and enjoy the banquet in celebration of your triumph."

I went silent and allowed myself to be dragged away until we were beneath the canopy together. I wondered why my mother would have protected the child of someone who hated her, but pushed it away as we sat and began to fill our plates. I ate at Rowan's side until my belly could fit no more. We laughed and drank spiced wine with the others until I had grown so flooded with exhaustion that my eyelids were practically cementing themselves shut. Rowan volunteered to accompany me to my quarters, which I readily accepted.

"Thank you," I said to him with a thick tongue. "For opening up to me tonight."

"Thank you, as well." He smiled, wrapping his arms in front of his chest as we approached the entrance.

"For what?"

"Caring." He said simply, allowing me to walk inside first. *Like a true gentleman.*

The moment we stepped into the castle, alcohol and fatigue were making me feel heavy. My limbs trembled as they struggled to take each step. Rowan promptly took notice and swept me up and into his muscular arms. He held me tight against his broad chest, walking in perfect soldier-like stride until he had eventually deposited me onto my bed. His brilliant eyes swept over my lips, and he turned to leave.

"Wait," I called after him softly, feeling much more awake, with the roaring desire inside being ignited anew. He swung his head around just enough to give me a smirk before walking through the door, leaving me alone in my thoughts. I knew that I needed to change out of the dress but didn't want to expend any more energy by getting some nightwear. I settled on removing the dress and throwing it into a heap on the floor, along with the bangles.

Sinking back into the mountain of pillows, all I could think about was Rowan and the kiss that had left me breathless. The way his body had pressed against mine...his cock. A bite of passion ached in my core. With a glance at the door, I traced my fingers down my breast, squeezing my nipples that had tightened at the memory of my rendezvous with Rowan.

When I arrived at my burning-hot slit, I panted at how ready I was, how close I was to plunging over the edge of the magnificent peak I stood on. Rowan's lustrous eyes observed me, in my subconscious, as I worked myself. I envisioned him thrusting that enormous cock into my delicate folds, while I slid one finger up and down on just the right spot and pushed another inside of my opening. A moan left my lips, and I felt my toes curling in. The world started to whirl, and my body convulsed in acknowledgment of the incoming orgasm.

Chapter Seventeen

Rowan

I RESTED IN BED, FULLY NAKED, NOT UNLIKE EVERY OTHER evening. No, something that made that night unusual was that my cock kept pulsating, thick against my taut abdomen, to the image of her. Being over a century in age, I'd had my fair share of partners, but nothing compared to the effect the Witch had on me. Something made her different from the rest. It was something that I couldn't put my finger on. The desire I felt when around her was like nothing I'd ever experienced before. I hungered for her.

Taking a firm grip on my length, I started to stroke it, up and down. I wished it was her fingers enveloping my cock as the pressure began to swell. I imagined her scent flooding into my nostrils, that Witchy smell of smoldering embers and alchemy components. But there lay something beneath that, something that smelled so foreign, yet so appealing. I needed that scent all over my skin.

I remembered how she had kissed me without hesitation and how I was so fucking pleased that she had done it. I craved to push her desire further than I ever had before. Further than anyone else that she had been with. All I could think of was ripping off that pretty dress to show her just how it felt to fuck a powerful Faery. She owned exactly what I needed, but I didn't want to scare her away...not again.

Stroking faster, I imaged putting my cock between those pretty lips and watching as she satisfied me on her knees. Tossing my head back, I prepared myself as the pull began to intensify, my entire body tense in anticipation.

"Eden," I growled her name through clenched teeth as the pleasure gushed from the tip of my dick and dripped down my fist. With a sigh of relief, I rose from the bed to wash. Despite the release, it was still taking every last drop of self-restraint to stop myself from returning to her chamber and fucking her until she was screaming my name. A rap on the door interrupted the impure thoughts. I swiveled to grab a blanket from the bed.

"What is it?" I called, binding it around my waist.

Azrael pushed his head into the crack of the door. The hard-ass look on his face was one that never left. Rightfully so, the guy was my most dependable warrior. There would be no one else that I'd have trusted to have my back like the seer. Closely related to a Witch, I didn't care. I viewed him as a weapon. A damn good sword, that loved nothing more than spilling the blood of those that wanted to fuck with me and mine.

"Sorry to bother you at this late hour, sire. But, you have a visitor. It's the Demon wench."

"Let her in," I spoke in a cold tone. Gods, I had grown so tired of Nija. The Trials couldn't be over soon enough. Once they were finished, she could go back to screwing any demon that was not myself. Fucking and sucking, it was what she did best. That might sound invigorating on the outside, but not when you know that you're bargaining with a succubus. The sex itself may be adequate, but the sucking only happens when she's devouring your soul.

"Good evening, my lord." Honey dripped from Nija's words. She wore a blood-red cloak that thumped against her ankles as she strode into my chambers.

"Feeding time already?" I already knew the answer; it was part of our contract. I had to feed her powers while keeping her safe and she could not wage war on my kingdom nor my allies. At least, not so long as she was with me. The contract extended further, but my thoughts drifted away from it at the sickeningly sweet tone of her voice.

"Am I interrupting something?" She asked with a wicked grin, her glowing eyes lingering a bit too long on my groin that still hadn't softened. Had I not been bred to be noble even in the presence of undesirables, I'd have told her to get the hell out and not come back. Breaking our agreement that way would require a dangerous lack of consideration for my people, though. So I bit my tongue while she swung her hips over to me.

"Not at all," I said, making my way to the chair sitting beside my table. There was no chance of me allowing her to climb into my bed with me, that would be too personal. After sitting down, I beckoned to her, which she all too eagerly went along with. I observed as she removed her hood, unveiling two twisted, black horns, expelling from each temple. She was weakened. Not only could I smell her Demonic power waning, but Nija wouldn't be caught dead sporting those things.

Her fingers seized both sides of the cloak, stretching it open casually, to exhibit her bare frame. Large wings that resembled a bat's hoisted at her back as both wiggled to release the cloak onto the floor. Gritting my teeth, I stared elsewhere while she mounted me, tearing the blanket away from my cock.

I felt no satisfaction in her guiding me against her slit and lowering until I was buried inside of her. I loathed that my body remained hard for her, even knowing it was at the will of her succubus energy. She was all business, though, as she worked to feed her strength while siphoning from my Demon side. She could take it all if she wanted, the only piece of a Demon *anything* that I cared for had been taken long ago. The thought reminded me of my conversation with Eden, which I swiftly forced away. As much as I'd love to be inside of the sexy little witch instead of the power-sucking pussy of Nija, it was wrong to think of her while fucking someone else.

Chapter Eighteen

THE LEATHER CORSET I WORE OVER THE BELL-SLEEVED SHIRT made creaking noises with every move that I made that morning. The matching leather pants that I had been required to use were doing exactly the same thing. The noise was creating a throb between my temples. I blocked out the noise as I tried, for a fourth time, to mount the gorgeous white mare I had been assigned. Slipping off of it, I cursed the stars and every single creation that had been put in this realm.

"Remind me again why I have to ride a fucking horse to this Trial?" I spat at Scott, who was standing nearby, smiling like an idiot while he watched me fail to get into the saddle. His arms were crisscrossed in front of him, a piece of straw wiggling across his lips where he nibbled on it.

"Because the location is too far to travel on foot," He said simply, plucking the hay from his trap and discarding it before walking over to lend a hand. *About fucking time.*

"Why can't they just magically transport us like last time?"

"I don't know Eden, presumably to spite you."

"Was that a joke?" I asked through narrowed eyes. Scott's face broke into a laugh as I climbed into his weaved hands so that he could hoist me onto the animal's back. As soon as my ass hit the saddle, I panicked and flung my arms around the throat of the beast. This was too freaking high in the air. Why did I have to do this? I'd never even been around horses in my life, let alone on the back of one.

"Are you going to ride her like that?" Scott asked with a raised eyebrow.

I squeezed my eyes shut and tightened my grip, feeling the massive muscles of the creature below me twitch in annoyance.

"I can't do this!" I whined, not caring that the other women could all see and hear me. Scott chuckled and patted my arm.

"You will be fine, she knows exactly where she is supposed to go. You might annoy her a little bit, clinging to her neck like that, but she will get you where you need to be."

"Annoy her?" I shouted, my eyes popping back open. "She's a freaking horse! Wasn't she bred and trained to tolerate people being on her back?"

"I've never had a problem with her." Scott shrugged and fiddled with the pouch at his hip. With a quick look around, he motioned for me to lean closer to him. Unsteadily, I did so and sat as still as possible while he pulled a silver chain with a small clear crystal dangling from it over my head.

"Tuck that into your--" His hands moved over his chest uncontrollably as he fought to avoid eye contact with me. "Your um..."

"You want me to put it in between my breasts?" I said with pursed lips and an elevated eyebrow. Glares from all around us snapped in our direction. I rolled my eyes and did as he had asked me to before anyone could get a good look at the necklace. Scott sighed in relief and gave me a single nod, smacking a fist into his opposite palm. "What is it for?"

"Shh!" He hushed me, looking around again. This time nobody cared; they were all too concerned with trying to figure out what exactly we were doing in the stables. Scott leaned close and spoke in a voice so low that I could only just hear him over the stomping of my horse's hooves. "It is a protection charm."

"Isn't that cheating?" I hissed, mimicking his tone.

"Not if you don't get caught with it," He said quietly, pretending to adjust the saddlebag that contained a waterskin and a grapple. The two items had me sweating. I didn't know how to rock climb, and if that was the challenge, I would *definitely* lose this one. "Good luck today, Eden."

"Someone had a bit too much wine this morning," I muttered as he walked away. Warily, I clutched two fists full of horse mane before attempting to straighten my spine. The horse huffed and bobbed her head at the change, but she didn't send me flying. I took that as a good sign.

"That's a good girl," I cooed at her. "See? We are bonding already."

"Good luck, Eden," Rowan said, walking in front of me. He had come from out of nowhere, like usual. I spoke a silent prayer of thanks, grateful that I had sat up before he saw me behaving like a wimp. He offered me a smile that melted my insides to a puddle as he began to make his way to the next woman.

"Yeah, you too!" I bit my tongue so hard that I tasted blood. *Fucking idiot,* I scolded myself inwardly while giving him my best smile. I watched Rowan grin and then make his way down the line, wishing everyone good luck before stepping onto the podium sitting in front of us.

"Good morning, competitors," He smiled and nodded to his right-hand man who held up a golden coin that glistened in the early sunlight. "Welcome to the second Trial. Today you will be facing the Trial of Cunning. You have presumably noticed that each of you is equipped with nothing more than water, a grappling set, and a horse. Each of these things could be of benefit to you in today's Trial." My eyes slid back to the coin as he motioned towards it.

"This is what you are after. A cave system lies to the south, one that you will each have to navigate to find the treasure. You may return when you have collected some of it. One piece, or one-hundred pieces, it does not matter. Your goal is to locate it, retrieve a portion, and bring it back here."

I nodded. It seemed easy enough. I caught sight of Shael, who had paled by at least a shade or two, her hands visibly trembling. Gulping against the forming lump in my throat, I tore my eyes away, trying to convince myself that she had probably eaten some bad eggs that morning. There was no way her behavior was related to what Rowan was explaining to us. *Nope, couldn't be.* With another glimpse, I noticed a dagger sheathed at her hip.

Shael returned my stare just as a horn blasted, sending my horse surging forth, into a hard run. I tightened my grip on her mane to keep my balance as my butt bounced on and off of the saddle. *Okay, I'm fine. I can do this.* Those were my thoughts but I was, in fact, not fine. My heart pounded in my ears as the horse galloped down the road alongside the others. Nija was in the lead, go figure. Closing my eyes for the first half, I couldn't bear to watch the dirt path flying under us at that speed.

I'm not sure how long the ride lasted, but I opened my eyes as we ran through a meadow and into more rocky terrain at the base of a mountain range. The sun was high in the sky, making the snow-capped mountains gleam as I scanned the scenery for the cave. My horse slowed, leaving us in the rear. I gave her a nudge with my heels, something I had seen people do in old westerns. She quickly swiveled her head around to stare at me with one large eye.

"Sorry," I scowled. "I thought you knew where we are supposed to be going?"

She whinnied in response and turned off the trail, swinging her head back around as she brought us to a stop in front of what looked to be a very large boulder. It seemed to have cracked in half, my guess was that it was probably a result of its fall down the mountainside. Swinging one leg over, I slid down her side and reached into the saddlebag to pull out the rest of my gear. With an awkward stroke to her neck and praise for getting me there alive, I left to begin searching the area.

The boulder was crushed tightly against the mountain's side. Narrowing my eyes against the sunlight, I could just make out a hole inside of it that looked big enough for me to crawl through. Wishing I had another one of Scott's illumination potions, I squeezed myself into the hole. Hot air clung to my face and arms the second I entered, and I had to remain crouched over as I made my way through. It continued to get hotter the further in I roamed. Placing my slick hands on the rock to steady myself, I noticed that the heat was coming off of the walls of my tunnel. Odd as this was, I continued forward, not seeing any other options.

Around a mile in, the shaft began to broaden, giving enough room for me to stand and walk comfortably. I continued to keep one hand firmly pressed against the wall, as I couldn't see a damn thing in front of me apart from a distant glow. I knew it to be light but couldn't tell if it was natural or firelight. Just. My boots were quiet beneath me, as I continued to make my way toward the dot and I tried to keep it that way, knowing I would be a sitting duck against the few others who came equipped with built-in night vision.

Finally, I approached a ledge that indicated the end of my entry tunnel. There was nowhere to go that I could see because the ledge dropped into a several-hundred-foot fall. I could detect light twinkling below so I fell to my belly as stealthily as possible, crawling forward so that I could peer over the edge. My breathing hitched in my chest at the scene beneath my shelter. Slapping a hand over my mouth to keep from screaming, I watched as the monstrous creature below exhaled laboriously.

The silvery scales of the beast glistened underneath the torch-light encircling it. Examining it from top to bottom, I could see that its enormous tail was curled in a semicircle around a heap of glittering-gold coins and a sprinkling of gems. The plumes emanating from its nostrils saturated the atmosphere with smoke swirls during each exhale, making it hard to take a satisfying inhale. My eyes grew wider as I noticed the petite figure of Shael moving around the creature's snout. She was backing away from Lavinia, causing them both to advance nearer to the dragon.

I couldn't make out what either of them was saying as they moved, but I could see the dagger glinting in Shael's hand, which indicated danger. My stomach flipped as gravel crumbled beneath a clawed foot beside them, making both of their heads twist to face the beast. The dragon was stirring, probably due to the two morons arguing by its head. I observed while the head of the creature rose, slowly turning to face them. Ear-splitting screams filled the air as the dragon's chest heaved, its neck and head rearing back for an attack. Helplessly, I watched as it opened its jaw, filling the cavern with molten flames.

A shimmering, sky-blue light spread over both of the women's bodies, though they still were knocked onto their backs from the force of the dragon's breath. I gawked, with an open mouth, as the two disappeared in a shower of sparks. Focusing my sights on my wrist, I witnessed two more points branding into it with searing discomfort. The pain was like thousands of white-hot pins marking my skin. How the hell was I supposed to get past that monster without the same thing happening to me? The sound of flapping wings reached my ears and I peered back into the cavern, expecting to see the dragon flying up to burn me to a crisp.

Instead, I followed Sephial with my cerulean stare as she gracefully soared over the dragon while it nestled back into the gold to continue its slumber. She ascended to the top of the cave before flipping backward smoothly, tucked her wings tightly against her body, and dropped in a nosedive. Plunging with experience and agility, she waited until the last possible second to spread her wings, coming to a complete stop just before smashing into the collection of riches.

A clawed foot snatched up as many gold pieces as could fit in it before Sephial gave a push with her colorful wings that sent gold pieces shooting out from under her and smacking into the thick, silver scales of the beast. She rose into the air once again, only *just* getting away before the dragon had time to react. I had no idea if Pimea and Nija had already completed the challenge, but I felt like I was running out of daylight. My mind spun, working to figure out how to get down, let alone past the dragon.

So far, my powers had taken a random variety of forms. I questioned if I would be able to harness something I hadn't before-- *earth*. Gazing up at the ragged stalactites lining the ceiling, I thought that if I could break one of those off, it might distract the dragon long enough for me to get down and grab a gold piece. Pulling the grappling hook and rope next to me, I fixed my sights on another ledge that was filled with large rocks. Those rocks would be a perfect place to launch my hook if I could throw it that far.

Pushing to my feet as silently as possible, I held the hook so that it was hanging from my right hand while unraveling the rope with my left. My intention was to get the grappling hook fastened securely so that, when I cast my spell, I would have the ability to swing down to the base of the cave. Glancing down at the area I'd land in, I estimated that it would likely be close enough for me to sprint, grab the gold, and get the hell out of this place. I gave myself a nod, trying to be confident that this would work.

Swinging the hook a few times, I made sure to hold onto the rope loosely enough to let it fly but hard enough so that I wouldn't lose it altogether. The hook soared through the air and smacked against a rock, scraping down the side of the ledge before falling.

"Shit," I muttered tugging the hook back up with the rope that I had tightened my grip on. "Second time's the charm, right?"

I tossed the hook out a second time, smirking and pulling tightly against the rope as it wrapped around my targeted stone.

Moving swiftly, I tied my end of the rope to my own ledge and spread my legs to settle into a good position for spellcasting. With a quick stroll down memory lane, I didn't feel anything more than a dull flickering inside of myself. Of course, when I needed my powers most, they weren't going to work for me. The shock of forcing myself to remember my mother's leaving didn't have the same effect this time.

I pushed harder, seeking to find anything that I could dredge up and make the flicker ignite into full-blown flames within my chest. Rowan came to mind in my search, how much I hated him to begin with and how it was starting to change the longer I stayed. A warmth passed through me as I began to recall every minute I spent with him...how my emotions were out of my control when near him. Tingling started in my fingers, making my heart lurch into my throat. This was doing it for me.

I peered up at the formations on the ceiling, focusing all of my energy on them. I remembered the previous night, seeing fireworks erupting overhead as I tiptoed to kiss him. His smile and how it felt pressed against my skin. The way his body had grown hard for me when we touched. Heat shot up through my center, bringing a wave of sensation with it. A rumbling quake started overhead, sending dirt and chunks of rock tumbling down around me. The stone started to shudder under my feet.

Fuck, I'm overdoing it. Trying to draw my power back in, I knew it was too late. The spell broke free with a *BOOM* and started to shatter everything around me, including the rock that held my escape tool. I scrambled to the rope, trying to grab hold of it before it slid over the edge. It was already gone, descending as the hook remained on platform number two. I didn't have time to mourn the loss as the next quake shook me violently, making it difficult to keep my footing. I felt my heart drop as a crumbling vibration started behind me.

Shifting to look, I released a single curse as the stone cracked and gave way. Accelerating down the slanted rock on my back, my body flipped over, landing me on my stomach. Scraping my finger-nails against the hard stone to try and find some type of purchase, I simultaneously pushing my boots against it, failing to grab hold of anything before my body was sent tumbling through barren air. I watched pieces of the cave falling from each side of me as I descended further and further until I finally crashed onto the ground, and the world glittered with a blue hue before going dark.

Chapter Nineteen

AWAKENING, I FELT A STABBING PAIN ON THE BACK OF MY head. Warmth trickled down my face. As I blinked the blood away and sat up, my muscles screeched at me to rest. I tried to disregard the agony riddling my body and looked around, identifying where I was and what had just happened. With sudden awareness, I shifted my sights in every direction quick enough to give myself whiplash, waiting for the dragon that would surely be above me at any second. A roar sent a chill deep into my bones. Just then, I spotted what I had been looking for. The Dragon appeared to be wounded, with blood pooling at its feet. I regarded the animal in horror as it tore at its eyes with claws larger than my body, attempting to protect them from the daylight that was now pouring into the cave. I knew I wouldn't have much time before those blazing-yellow eyes settled on me to seek revenge.

Stumbling to my feet, I forced my body forward and toward the pile of gold that the dragon's tail was thrashing around in. The best that I could do was hobble at it and pray that the tail didn't lash out in my direction, knowing I wouldn't have the strength to dodge it. The dragon caught sight of me just as I stretched my arm out to pluck a gold piece from its resting place. Our eyes met and my adrenaline kicked into overdrive. Stuffing the coin into my pocket, I flipped around and limped as fast as I could manage away from the creature that was now very aware of my presence.

A ticking noise from deep within the throat of the creature sounded through the cave, prompting me to shoot a glance over my shoulder. Seeing the overgrown lizard stepping closer to me, I watched as acidic flames started to mix with the blood dribbling from its snout. I snapped my head back around and searched desperately for some sort of exit. *There.*

Bolting to the left, I managed to squeeze myself into a tall split in the cave wall just as the flames discharged from the muzzle of the monstrosity. The heat from the dragon's blaze forced me to turn my head away for fear of my face melting off. My right arm got the worst of it and I felt every blister as they formed on my fingers and over half my chest. Pain wasn't present, most likely because of the shock flowing through me. The sleeve of my shirt caught fire, but I didn't stop to put it out, my focus was getting to the opening on the opposite side.

The rough stone dug into my chest and back as I pushed myself through. Once on the other side, my knees gave out. All I could remember was falling onto my face and then darkness again.

❧

"EDEN!" THE VOICE OF AN ANGEL CALLED TO ME, FORCING MY eyes open. Pimea had her hands under my armpits as she dragged me from the cave. My tongue was too thick, too coated in hot blood, to speak. Moving my hand up to my neck, a fleeting thought told me to remember to thank Scott for the protection amulet once we returned. My hand came up empty, I must have lost the necklace in the fall. Pimea's terrified eyes started to sharpen in my blurry vision.

"How the hell did you become so wounded?" She hissed. I

could feel her anger as it fell from her lips. The frustration wasn't directed at me. "There are protection spells in place for a reason! You could have..." Her voice went quiet for a moment.

"Never mind that we need to return you to the castle. Lord Blaive has the best healers in the realm at his disposal. Just hold on, okay?"

I nodded at her as best as I could, not even sure if my head was moving at all. Closing my eyes, I couldn't stop the dark fog from entering my vision and pulling me down.

When I opened them again, I could hear hushed voices all around me. They sounded urgent. One was deep and angry. He was yelling about something. The world began to spin and I felt my body respond by trying to expel the contents of my stomach.

"Get her on her side, you fools, she's about to vomit." The voice belonged to Rowan. "If she dies, I will have all of your fucking heads on stakes."

I opened my mouth and heaved until my belly was empty. Soft hands touched me, cutting the fabric that had become fused with my skin free as they worked on healing my broken body. I was in and out for most of the process, only catching bits and pieces of conversations between the sleep cycles.

"I want you to find out how the fuck this happened Azrael, you know what is at stake if word of this gets out. These women are under the crown's protection during the Trials." Rowan's voice sounded tight and pissed off. "Figure it out. Do it now."

"Yes, sire," Rumbled the deepest voice I'd ever heard. It must have belonged to the one he was calling Azrael. With that, I heard footsteps as the second person left. A gentle, cool hand pressed against my throbbing forehead as I lay there, trying to force my eyes to open.

"Hold still if it hurts," Rowan purred at me. Able to lift my lids just enough to see him, I gave a sheepish smile and pushed my hands against the soft surface below me, attempting to raise into a sitting position. I winced and fell back against the pillow. I didn't hurt as I had before the healing, it was more like the feeling you get when you first start intense exercising. Sore muscles, a headache, and the constant need to throw up. "Damn it, woman, I said to lay still."

"I don't take orders from you, Rowan." I croaked, watching his lips twitch into a grin. I was able to pull my eyes open the rest of the way in just enough time to realize that I was completely naked, lying on his bed. My hands flew to the blanket, tugging it up around my shoulders while Rowan chuckled in the chair sitting beside me, blotting the remainder of dried blood from my face.

"Calm yourself, princess, all the important parts were covered by my healers."

"Thank goodness for that," I muttered and groaned as a sharp pain pierced my lungs. "How long was I out?"

"You've been asleep, on and off, since you were returned to the castle yesterday evening."

I slept for a full night and then some...in Rowan's bed. I tried not to think about how long he had been in there with me. Naked. And covered in blood.

"What happened? I'm not supposed to die here, right?"

Rowan sighed and shook his head, causing his dark curls to dance around his chin. His pale eyes had grown dark and were focused on the bed, avoiding my stare. The sight of his rugged hair and beautiful face was getting me a little too excited. I was used to seeing him all prettied up. This was a different side of him, one that was less tame. And damn sexy.

"We don't know yet. You should have been protected from the fall-"

"How did you know I fell?" I asked.

"Your friend, the Siren, saw it happen just as she was going for the gold as well. She said she doesn't know how you made it out, and frankly, neither do my healers. You should have died, Eden." His voice was kind but firm, his eyes flicked to mine. "She also said she needed to speak with you. Alone. I assured her that she could wait until you were feeling up to it."

"Maybe I inherited some of my mother's healing powers." I shrugged, sending another ripple of pain over my body. I'd deal with whatever Pimea needed when I was able to walk on my own. "Ouch."

"Perhaps. We can figure that out at a later time. For now, are you all right? The healers did what they could without killing themselves by exerting too much energy."

"Feeling peachy, thanks," I said with a lopsided grin. Rowan rose from the chair, shifting to the edge of the bed so that he could tug one of my hands away from the blanket under my chin. I let him move it, not that I had the energy to fight him, and watched as he softly trailed his fingers up and down my forearm.

"I'm glad," Rowan said, audibly swallowing. "That you survived, that is."

"You and me both, buddy." I let out a sigh and relaxed into his touch. I didn't want him to stop. Closing my eyes, I could feel sleep tugging at me, beckoning me to fall back into dreamland. I almost did, too, until Rowan softly pressed his lips against mine. A flurry of feelings hit my abdomen as I moved my lips with his in a perfectly sweet tempo. I lifted my other hand to cup his chiseled jaw, feeling it tighten with each stroke of his tongue against mine.

Pulling back, my lips remained parted for his as I gazed into his intense stare from beneath my lashes. His thumb caressed my cheek, and he breathed out heavily like a weight had been lifted from his shoulders. I could feel the sexual tension flickering in a threat to leave me completely as I let my head fall back against the soft pillow. My body ached in more ways than one. Falling from several hundred feet would do that to a person. So would not getting laid when you really wanted to.

"I'd kill for a hot bath right now," I murmured. Rowan's eyes lit up, and that familiar smirk spread across his face. It made me feel like a giddy teenager. The cute boy from fourth period was looking at me, and I didn't know what to do other than blush.

"Why didn't you say so sooner?"

With that, he was off of the bed and making his way to a door that I hadn't noticed the first time I had been in his room. Probably because he had been on top of me for the majority of it. Pausing to turn around, he watched as I struggled against the pain in my rib cage and right leg to sit up. Making sure I had the blanket covering all of my most intimates, I wasn't surprised when he returned to help me.

"Drop the blanket, I'm not looking if you don't want me to." He said firmly. I trusted that he was telling the truth, it was written all over his face. It wasn't that I didn't want him to look, I did. I just wanted to be a little less dirty when he did. "I would never do anything that you disagreed with. I promise you that."

"What if I do want it?" The words had slipped from my thoughts and formed on my tongue before I could stop them. My head bowed as the prickling heat of a flush spread across my cheeks. Rowan took my chin in between his thumb and forefinger, pulling it up so that I was looking into those magnificent eyes of green.

"Anything you desire shall be yours. But maybe when you are less... covered in filth." His voice was like silk in my ears, making it hard to tell if that was a compliment or an insult. Either way, I was melting in his grasp, becoming nothing more than a puddle of longing. I chuckled nervously as he released my chin and moved his arms underneath me gently, letting the blanket fall away as he lifted me from the bed and took me into his bathing room. Allowing my head to rest against his chest, I could feel his warmth soaking into me and reveled in it. His heart strummed in his chest to a steady, strong rhythm.

Once we had entered the bathing room, he set me down on a deep blue, velvet-cushioned bench. The walls were white and made of a stone that I didn't recognize. Stained glass windows illuminated the room with bright daylight in hints of teal and aqua. I shifted with a grunt to get a better look at the enormous bathtub.

It looked like a giant bowl, one that was made of pure marble. There was no faucet or other sources of water leading into it, which I quickly discovered the reasoning for. Rowan held his open palms over the tub, whispering something under his breath. Watching in awe, I couldn't help but be impressed as clean water began to fill the tub. And, even better, it was steaming with warmth. Not needing his hands over it for the spell to continue, Rowan moved to several decanters full of luxurious soaps and poured two honey-colored bottles into the tub.

Inhaling, I breathed in the smell of sweet oats and fresh berries that came to me, wafting through the steam. Rowan moved back, holding a hand out to help me. I let him pull me up and stopped before setting a foot into it.

"Join me?" I breathed.

"Eden, if I get into this tub with you, I won't be able to hold myself back. I'd break you, more than you already are. Let me wash you, and we will see how you feel afterward, alright?"

Disappointed, I nodded and proceeded to enter the sinfully soothing water. Rowan took both of my hands and lowered me until my butt hit the bottom. Laying against the side, most of my body was submerged beneath a heap of bubbles. I let myself relax and enjoyed every sensation as the hot water absorbed into my bruised muscles.

"How does it feel?" He questioned while pouring more soap into his hands and working it into a thick lather. I moaned a little as he began to rub it into my shoulders and upper back, moving down my arms.

"It feels like heaven," I whispered as my eyes rolled back. His breath hitched as he moved his hands up my arms, and his knuckles grazed the side of my breast that was slick with soapy water. Moving on from it swiftly, he washed my hair and moved onto my feet which were a little worse for wear at that point. He didn't seem to mind scrubbing them until the grime had all been removed. When he had finished, he grabbed a fluffy towel from its perch and held it open in front of himself.

I carefully placed my hands on the edge and lifted myself with the stealth of a ninety-year-old woman and let him wrap me in the fine towel. We shuffled back into the room where a silken emerald gown with a plunging neckline and strappy back awaited me on the side of the bed. I didn't question how it had gotten there; magic was always the answer here. Rowan didn't hesitate to grab it and helped me get dressed. Every brush of his skin against mine sent new waves of heat into my core. Unfortunately, my body was far too exhausted after the short trip to the bath. I climbed into the bed and let my eyes close. Rowan watched me the whole time, beginning to take his place in the chair once again.

"Lay by me," I whispered with a yawn. Not having to ask twice, I felt his massive body climb into the bed behind me. Rowan drew the blankets over my shoulders and nestled his face against the nape of my neck. His warmth soaked into my blood, making me feel even more fatigued. My heart slowed as we lay there, just breathing in perfect sync. Sleep came for me, despite my fighting it.

A hand slid over the skin of my thigh, causing me to gasp awake. The pain in my body had nearly gone completely, I regarded Rowan's eyes, which were gleaming emeralds as he looked at me hungrily while I rolled over to face him. Twilight had fallen outside of the windows, and the blaze in the hearth lit the room dimly with a soothing series of crackles and pops. I brought a hand up to caress the Elf's face and pull it against mine.

Rowan kissed me intensely, his fingers dipping beneath the dress and up my hip. Realizing I wasn't wearing any undergarments, my heart fluttered. His lips tasted of desire, I explored the flavor with my tongue as my nipples stiffened, straining against the silk gown.

"I need to be inside of you Eden, I can't wait any longer. Please, allow me..." He growled against my lips. I nodded in approval, my need was just as prominent as his own. Continuing to kiss and suckle at his lips, I moved my feet apart to allow him entrance. Rowan received my answer and pushed his hand between my thighs. Soaking wet downstairs, and panting like a dog, my chest heaved as he thrust a single finger deep inside of me. His breathing hitched at the feeling of my desire, which set fire to my passion. Moaning in response, I watched his eyes that blazed with the same desire.

"You're so wet, so tight...so ready for me." He growled, becoming the predator hunting his prey once again. Driving a second finger into my folds, I gasped and let my head fall back in pleasure. He began to move them in and out slowly, expanding the need through my abdomen and thighs. With his thumb, he worked to tease my clitoris, nearly sending me over the edge.

"Not yet, Witch." He commanded, removing his fingers from me and moving to where his head was between my thighs. I let them fall open, fully revealing myself to him. There was a momentary lapse in his authoritative nature as he studied me. "Gods, you're perfect," he breathed.

"I want to taste you, is that alright?"

I bent forward without a word. Spreading my fingers through his thick curls, I took hold of his hair and guided his face exactly where I wanted it to be. He smiled up at me coyly and began to kiss my center with his soft lips. I moaned and arched my back as he flicked his tongue over my core, sucking on it lightly before replacing his fingers inside of my pussy. Waves of need washed over me as he got into a rhythm, stroking my slit and curling his fingers inside, just enough to hit the spot.

"I want your release in my mouth," He said in a husky voice that sent another burst of moisture dripping from my sex. "Come for me, Eden."

The sound of my name leaving his lips drove me over the

edge. My body started to shake, sucking his fingers even deeper inside as I cried out in sheer ecstasy. His head dropped as he extracted his fingers from me carefully so that he could lap up every last drop of my lust. I brushed my fingers through his hair as he did so, only allowing them to fall back to the bed when he lifted himself to kiss me, the taste of my passion sweet and glossy on his lips.

He let his body sink against mine, his kiss gentle as he took my lips between his, one at a time, sucking them softly. His firm cock pushed against my belly button making me gulp. He was huge. I wasn't sure I'd be able to take his full length. I started to reach down, to return the favor but a stab in my wrist stopped me. The familiar sensation disturbed me, this wasn't the place for a point to burn itself into my skin.

"Wait," I said, moving out from underneath Rowan. "Something is wrong."

Like clockwork, there was an urgent rapping on the door. I looked to Rowan in panic. He got up to answer the door while I righted my clothing. Azrael marched through the entrance that Rowan had pulled open, his eyes momentarily connecting with mine before he got down to business. I felt almost violated by his eyes, like he knew every detail of what had just happened.

"My Lord, one of the participants, has been eliminated while she slept." He said matter-of-factly.

"What?" Rowan bellowed, his voice full of rage. "By whom?"

"We do not know, sire."

"Fuck!" Rowan shouted, his deep voice almost sounding distorted as anger flushed his face. He paced for a minute before stopping in front of his guard and raking a hand through his disordered hair. "Which female?"

"The Siren, Pimea, your grace."

My heart sank at the sound of her name.

Chapter Twenty

"Strangulation was the cause of death, sire." Azrael and Rowan went over the briefing as I choked back sobs, resting on the edge of the bed. Pimea had saved my life, she had pulled my broken and bloodied body back here to get help. She had also been the only person besides Scott to try befriending me since arriving in the Fae Realm. I couldn't believe that she was gone and that I hadn't taken the time to get to know her better.

Anger and sadness rippled through me in chaotic harmony, sending surges of power to my fingertips. I wanted to find who did it, to rip their heart from their chest while they still breathed. Working to conceal it, before either of the men caught on that I was about to explode into flames, I looked up at Rowan.

"Can I use your restroom?" I asked in a trembling voice. He nodded to me, his eyebrows drawing together with concern. I strode into the bathroom, closing the door behind me just in time for flames to burst from my palms. Racing to the mirror, I was planning on calming myself with a pep talk. When I approached, however, the tears running down my cheeks had caught flames, like gasoline.

"Fuck," I seethed and slapped at the fire, attempting to extinguish it. After several deep breaths, I finally succeeded in snuffing them out. It was just in time for someone to tap softly on the door. I wiped the mess from underneath my eyes with the back of my hand and swung the door open. Rowan stood there looking like a kicked puppy.

"What's wrong?" I sniffled.

"You are to be confined to your quarters until further notice," Rowan spoke quietly like he was being forced to do something that he had no control of. A movement behind his shoulder caught my eye. I drove my way past him, examining his lowered eyes until I could no longer see them. Scott was standing in the room, an expression of full-blown rage on his tight face.

"With me. Now, Eden," he said, thrusting a finger at the door. I glanced back at Rowan, who had shifted and narrowed his eyes at Scott. The look was one of pure hatred, but he didn't speak out against it. Feeling very much like a teenager being caught with her boyfriend after hours, I bowed my head and walked to where Scott pointed. He trailed behind, seizing my arm as he walked me hurriedly to my room.

"You don't have to hold my arm that way, Scott. It isn't like I'm going to run away from you. What the hell is going on?"

"Oh, I don't know." He said, elbowing me into my room and closing the door behind us. My eyes were wide with confusion as I looked back at him after nearly falling from the force of his shove.

"Perhaps it has something to do with a girl dying at the hands of an unnamed criminal. Or possibly, I'm angry because my student, my queen-to-be, is too busy mating with the prince after nearly dying, to make sure to tell me she is okay. Did you even consider me afterward, Eden? I was concerned about you!"

My throat constricted as he filled the distance between us, taking a fistful of hair at the back of my neck. I jerked a hand up, alarm prompting my spell to begin forming. With a skillful move, Scott seized my wrist and dragged it back down to my side.

"What's wrong, princess?" He asked, his eyes wild, burning brightly in their sockets. "Too good for your own kind?"

"Scott, stop," I said with trembling lips, sensing tears falling onto my cheeks.

"He doesn't love you, you know that, right? To him, you are just a *Witch*. Filth, dirt, grime beneath his boots. He wants to take you as he does with the Demon you fight against. You do know that, don't you? That he calls her to his room every night so that he can fuck her?"

"I'm asking you to stop," I whimpered as he tightened his grip, pulling my hair so that my neck was exposed to him. I flinched against his touch as he began to kiss my neck, rough with anger and frustration. His hand freed my wrist and darted up to the delicate strap on my shoulder. I cried out as he ripped it apart, exposing more of my flesh.

"Rowan," I whispered without understanding why, as the sapphire tint overtook my vision for a split-second. All I knew was that I needed him to be here, to stop this, as I didn't have the strength or know-how.

"He isn't here, Eden. And you won't be accompanying him again. I'll be arranging transport to get you back to the Coven tonight. While you are there, you can think about marrying someone who *does* love you, someone like me—"

With a splintering crack, the door banged open and split into pieces that tumbled to the floor. Rowan marched in, his shoulders heaving as his violently glowing eyes landed on Scott. With one hand, he hoisted the male Witch into the air and sent him flying into the wall behind me. Rowan's eyes trailed down my body, lingering on my chest. I glanced down to see that one of my breasts was completely exposed and hastily covered myself before moving behind my savior. Rowan's eyes heeded me, his jaw clenching until he was sure that I was safely within his reach.

"I'll fucking kill you, Witch." He roared at Scott, who was scrambling to his feet. Electricity swirled in the air; I could feel the tension of their separate powers clashing against each other. Rowan moved with ease to the other side of the room, picking Scott up by the throat. I could hear Scott laboring to inhale as Rowan's hand began to tighten, slowly crushing his windpipe.

"Rowan, don't, please," I screamed. Rowan glanced at me and then looked back up to Scott. His body wavered in hesitation, as though it was taking every ounce of concentration not to finish the job.

"If I see your worm face anywhere in the seven kingdoms again, I will remove your head from your body." With that, he flung Scott to the side like a ragdoll. Azrael jogged up behind me, pushing past my trembling frame to enter the room.

"Your Grace, I apologize. I didn't sense that you were leaving."

"Take this trash to the border and toss him into the wilds. He can find his people without our help."

I gazed at Scott sorrowfully, watching the blood dribble from his nose. The look on his face was no longer rage, it was regret. I felt sad for him, wishing that I hadn't troubled him the way that I had. Azrael obeyed his Prince, yanking Scott to his feet by the collar of his coat and removing him from my room. I didn't look Scott in the eye as they passed by. But I could sense his grief as it flowed through him. I wanted to weep with my eyes locked on the mess of splintered wood on the floor.

"You are staying in my room tonight," Rowan ordered, making me look back up. "I'm not letting you out of my sight now."

Rowan strode to my wardrobe, extracting a lavish robe and draping it over my shoulders. He also grabbed a replacement dress and led me back to his room. Thankfully, the halls were deserted, as the castle was on lockdown. Once we were safely back in his room, I changed clothes and crawled into the bed, letting the emotions pour out of me. Rowan held my hand in silence as I let it all out.

Sniffing back tears, I eventually wiped my face with the handkerchief Rowan provided at some point and looked at him apologetically.

"Sorry," I croaked, my voice weak from sobbing. "It's just been kind of a crazy day, you know?"

"Don't apologize, Eden. None of this is your fault."

"Maybe not. I can't help but notice that I either drive people away or make them want to hurt me. From my mother leaving, and my father dying of cancer, Pimea getting killed, and then Scott attacking me the way that he did. Not to mention, I was a total bitch to Benjamin when all he wanted was a date," I snorted. "I'm fucking tainted. Ruined."

"No, you're not," Rowan said in a tone softer than I had ever heard come out of his mouth. "You are loving and courageous. Not to mention, stunning from head to toe. Please, don't be upset."

"What would you know?" I replied dejectedly, shaking my head as I wiped my nose on the cloth. "You don't know me at all."

"I know that you care for others, Eden. Even when that Witch attacked you, I saw in your eyes that you felt responsible. You feel responsible for your mother leaving, and for having to leave your sister and your father." He moved closer, his head low as the next words rumbled from his chest with such sincerity that I almost started bawling again.

"I'm so sorry, Eden. If I could take it all back, I would. Had I felt for you in the beginning, the way that I do now, I would have surrendered every pleasing moment that I've had with you, to spare you from all of this pain that you are feeling."

"How you feel about me?" I snorted. As much as I had tried to take Scott's words with a grain of salt, I couldn't shake what he had said. "You and Nija are doing stuff behind the scenes, so I've heard. I'm nothing more than a pawn--"

"You're wrong." Rowan's eyes were hard and cold. "You know naught of what you speak. Nija is a means to an end. One that I'm beginning to reconsider."

"I don't even know what that means," I rolled my eyes and rubbed my temples. Rowan took my hand in his, stroking the back of it with his thumb. I remembered what else he had stroked with that thumb, earlier...

"I don't enjoy taking her; you must understand that. Nija needs to feed on power, she would die without it. Being a part of these Trials, she has no other choice in a source. My people are at war with hers, I must accommodate her while she is in my care."

"So," I swallowed against the dryness in my throat. "The sex with her is a transaction?"

"Precisely," Rowan replied grimly. "Eden, I--"

He stopped, lowering his eyes to the floor. It was strange to see him this way, so exposed and vulnerable with his feelings. Nothing like the hard-ass Fae prince I had met several days ago. I placed my fingers under his chin, lifting it so that his gaze was on me again, encouraging him to continue. His lips twitched at the corners, a nervous grin showing ever-so-slightly.

"Eden," He cleared his throat and I could feel his hands begin to shake in mine. Puffing out a breath of air, he glanced at the table, trying to find a distraction. "I think that you should eat something. You need strength for the Final Trial tomorrow."

"That's all you wanted to tell me?" I asked quietly, seeing in his eyes that there was more. I tried to sift through the feelings emanating from him, but he had walls up, and I didn't know how to control my empathic side. My belly growled on cue, shifting the mood as if to prove what he was saying was what he meant all along. Knowing better, my head lowered and I nodded. "Okay, I'll eat something. Then we can finish this conversation. Right?"

Rowan agreed and snapped his fingers, summoning a servant into the room. She popped out of thin air with a *whoosh*, which sent me falling backward onto the bed.

"Food," Rowan said simply. The servant bowed, eyeing me nervously before running out of the entrance. We waited in silence for her to return. She reappeared promptly, pushing a trolley full of various silver trays. Most of them held berries, bread, and cheese. Plus, a few bottles of wine and other spirits. After placing them on the table, which was several sizes larger than the one in my chamber, she bowed again and left in a hurry.

"Please," Rowan motioned at the table. As much as I wanted to just forgo the eating and get right to the nitty-gritty, my stomach had other ideas. I yielded, walking to the table to sit and eat till my belly was full and content. Rowan sat across from me, nibbling on bits and pieces of fruit. I got the impression that he was only doing it to make me feel more comfortable, not because he was hungry. Rubbing my hands together after I tossed down the apple core I'd been gnawing on, my back fell against the chair.

"Okay, I ate. Now let's talk."

He seemed conflicted. Like something was simmering under the surface, struggling to get out. My eyes tracked him as he moved from the chair, holding out a hand for me. I caught it so that he could pull me up in front of his chest. Drawing me tight in an embrace, Rowan held me against himself for several moments before speaking. Leaning me back so that he could look into my eyes, he smiled sweetly, making me want to forget about our talk altogether just so that I could kiss him until sunrise.

"I want you to be mine," he said slowly, sweeping a finger across my forehead to remove a stray hair. "It is wrong for someone in my position to take sides. But...I want you to win the Trial. I've never met anyone like you before, and--" His Adam's apple bobbed as he swallowed hard, his eyelashes drooping under my stare.

"I demand to have you as my queen."

I could hardly feel my breath as it left my chest. I wanted him too, god knows I did. And I couldn't even explain why. Everything inside of me told me to hate him, to kick and scream until he sent me away. He was everything that I'd always been afraid of. A perfect man. It scared me to death. But it was more than that. My desire for him was untamed, I couldn't explain it if I tried.

"You don't have to feel the same, Eden. I just needed to tell you. Now you know-"

"I feel the same," I said, not able to keep staring into his piercing gaze. "I know that I shouldn't. I know that it is wrong. But I can't help how I feel. When I'm with you, things feel right. In ways that I can't explain."

A smirk broke out across his face in my peripherals, making my heart stutter. Was it really so crazy to Rowan that a weak nobody could care about him the way I did? His hand lifted to caress my cheek, luring me to his lips with a soft kiss.

"What if I fail?" I breathed, dread gripping my gut tightly. "What if I'm bested, and then you are lost to me forever? I won't know what to do..." Tears stung my eyes, dropping me in a puddle of uncertainty. Didn't I want to go home, to be with my family? What the fuck was wrong with me, talking like this was my new home? As though I could just forget where I came from. I guess a part of me *wanted* to leave it all behind.

"You won't fail," Rowan said stubbornly. I gazed at his face with pure admiration, tracing every feature with my eyes. How could he have so much faith in me when days ago he had wanted nothing more than for me to fail?

"Would I be able to bring my family here? You have healers, they could care for my father, couldn't they?"

"There are rules here, Eden," Rowan said in a kind tone that masked what he was telling me. "Your sister is unknown to us right now, but your father is not Faekind. If you were to bring him here, he wouldn't be able to return. Is that something he would agree to?"

"Maybe," I shrugged, resisting the tears forming in my eyes again as I pushed away to sit at the foot of the mattress. "I can't leave them behind, Rowan."

"And I cannot be without you," he replied, sitting beside me and wrapping a muscular arm around my waist. His hand gripped my thigh. "I stand by what I said before, anything you desire shall be yours. As my Queen, you would have anything you could ask for, your family included. My healers aren't entirely unfamiliar with human illness. They may be able to treat your father."

"Thank you," I sighed, feeling that the stone that had been weighing heavily on my heart was finally lifted. The pieces of the puzzle were crashing into place around me. Rowan's grip on my thighs tightened, provoking a burning in my belly.

I wanted this.

Wanted *him*.

I knew that after everything we said, everything we'd done, there was no going back. This moment—if we acted on it—would solidify this connection we shared.

I should walk away, because there are no guarantees, especially in my dark king's world. But instead, I lean in.

I give in.

Knowing full well I may never recover.

Chapter Twenty-One

Rowan pulled up the pale blue dress around me with his fingers and stood to remove it.

Grabbing his tunic's buttons in my own hands, I moved with the urgency that was building inside of me to undo them. Pulling open his white shirt, it revealed a flawlessly chiseled torso, taut with muscles.

"Dear God," I muttered, feeling myself growing moist. He allowed me to unbutton his pants, waiting as I dropped to my knees in front of him. My fingers fumbled with the clasp. He smothered a roguish grin and brought his hands up to assist me. I sighed in relief as the last button popped open, allowing me to drag the pants down so that his cock sprang up, slapping against his belly. Holy fucking huge dick, I thought with a drying throat.

"I want you in my mouth." I gulped, looking up through my lashes at him.

"Whatever you wish," he whispered with the grin still on his beautiful face.

Grasping the shaft of his enormous cock in one hand, I guided him inside of my mouth, feeling him swell against my cheeks as I sucked him softly. His length slid up my slick tongue inch by inch until it pressed against the back of my throat. I drew back, feeling his body tense as I flicked my tongue just underneath the head, teasing him before pushing him into me again. There was no way I was going to get the entire thing in this way, but I was sure as fuck going to try.

I continued to bob my head on him, gently twisting and pumping with my hand as I sucked and tongued every curve of him until pre-come beaded at the tip of his dick. It tingled in my mouth, a perfect mixture of salty and sweet. Rowan's fingers raked through my hair as his orgasm swelled within, pushing himself a little further than I could with each thrust of his hips. My cheeks were full of him and it felt right, like I was the lock and he was the key. Seafoam eyes never left mine as his pushes grew urgent, his eyebrows drawing together while the release slid from him and onto the back of my tongue and down my throat.

A deep, growling moan left his lips as he came, making the wet between my legs increase. Once the shaking in his thighs had come to a stop, I finished sucking him and slowly drew my head back, giving him one last tease with my tongue before he dropped from my lips. The sensation made him shudder and moan again. I presumed that he would lose the stiffness in his dick, but instead, he gazed at me with burning eyes and drew me up with his arms, laying me flat on my back atop the bed.

Rowan swept his fingers across my skin, tracing from my lips to my neck and my breasts. He cupped them as his tongue flicked over my nipples, making them stiff with yearning. Encircling his lips around one, he started to suck and moved a finger to my mons. I was dripping wet for him, he easily slid in two fingers to spread me open, preparing me for the large cock throbbing against his belly.

"I need you inside of me," I gulped as my delicate muscles ached around his fingers. He smiled wickedly, removing his fingers and shoving my thighs apart so that he was positioned between them. Leaning forward, I moaned at the feeling of his cock sliding up against my folds. The tip kissed my center, not yet entering it. I began to squirm with need.

"I'm going to fuck you until you scream my name, do you understand?" He growled, sending a shiver up my spine.

"Yes, oh God, yes, *please*." I panted, grinding my hips to try and force him further inside. I needed it, more than I had ever needed anything in my life. What was the air when I had him? He thrust against me but not hard enough to penetrate. It was another tease, payback for my teasing him. Rowan smiled and slid his cock over my clitoris, knowing that he was already close to sending me over the edge by the way I was fidgeting. I wanted to beg. To promise him anything, so long as he finished what he had started.

"Ready, Witch?"

He didn't give me time to answer as he pushed himself inside of my aching slit. I couldn't so much as breathe with every marvelous inch of him that was entering me. His cock grew against the smooth walls of my vagina, stretching me out until I wasn't sure if I would be able to take anymore. His neck was rigid, his breathing shallow, as though it was having the same impact on him as it was me. He looked so beautiful. Shoving his hands under my waist, he dragged my back into an arch so that he could bury himself in my pussy even further.

I cried out in satisfaction, which was cut short by his lips pressing against mine. It was the calm before the storm. Rowan adjusted his hips and started to rock back and forth, my muscles pulling him deeper. Releasing my lips from his, he stood tall on the floor while my ass hung halfway off of the bed. He used one hand to tweak my nipples and the other to massage my core. It was almost too much to take. Waves of pleasure sloshed around me until my ears were ringing.

With every thrust, his cock slammed against my inner walls, which suckled at him, wanting more. Rowan was eager to give it.

"Gods, you are fucking perfect." He said between breaths. I

could do nothing but pant in response, the need inside of me rising. I was a screaming teapot about to bubble over. The wave was going to come crashing down, sending me into another plane of existence. No lover I'd ever had, had made me feel the way that I did at that moment. It was like my own personal shard of heaven, and the angels were singing as I felt my inner muscles tighten around Rowan. "You're mine. I own you now. Every time you orgasm, it will be because of me. Do you understand?"

Rowan thrust a hand under my head to pull my forehead against his, still buried inside of my opening. He wasn't even sweating.

"Yes," I breathed in gasps as my body decreased in its shivering. I didn't take the words lightly. I was his. And, shockingly, the idea of it didn't make me want to leave. My thoughts were disrupted as he slammed his hips against my ass, shoving himself into me as far as he could. So deep that I bit my lip in a wonderful mixture of pain and pleasure. He continued the dance of pulling out to where his tip rested just inside of my opening and then thrusting so strongly that I thought I might split in two.

With swift hands, he flipped me onto my stomach and plowed himself into me deeper than before. I took the blanket between my teeth to stop myself from screaming. Rowan noticed the attempt to stifle my voice and leaned forward to take a handful of my hair, pulling me back so that he could kiss my neck, never stopping his perfect rhythm. The quilt fell from my lips, leaving my mouth wide open, my brows drawn in ecstasy.

He kept me that way, enjoying inflicting the small amount of pain just as much as I was enjoying feeling it. His cock grew even more solid inside of me, making every thrust feel so much harder. My eyes rolled back, and my teeth were bared, clenching tightly.

"Yes, baby! Please give me all of you, Rowan!" I screamed through my teeth, releasing the pent-up cries that were begging to be set free. It was what Rowan had been waiting for. He pulled himself from me just in time, and I felt his come roll over my hips and flow in hot droplets down my belly. With one snap of his fingers, a towel appeared in his hand and he started to wipe me clean. When he had finished, he tossed it to the floor and turned me to face him.

A flush crept up my neck and across my chest when I saw his eyes. They were bright, so full of pleasure that it made me feel more naked than ever. Rowan trailed his hands down my shoulders, across the crevasse of my inner elbows and into my hands, entangling his fingers with mine.

"I think--" I breathed, trying to muster some courage. With a sigh, I thought, *fuck it*. What did I have to lose? Besides possibly the only being I'd developed intense feelings for, in this world or my own. "I think that I'm falling for you, Rowan. I'm sorry, I can't help but feel connected to you somehow"

"Eden," He answered, drawing my chin up so that I was looking at my fears, straight in the face. Rowan's gaze slid from my chin to my lips and rested on my eyes. "I've known you'd destroy me from the moment we met. You are like nothing I have been trained to expect. I'm captivated by you. My mind turns itself over to the point of utter confusion every time that we touch. A woman like you is a rare find, no matter what Realm you belong to. I'd be a fool not to feel the same."

I wanted to weep at the understanding that coated his words, and I knew he had meant every single one of them. A memory uprooted me from the bliss of that moment as I wondered how much of the emotional whirlwind I had just felt was my own, and how much of it was his. Scott had said that I had absorbed his emotions when I attacked him. It made me wonder how much of the lust had been my own. How much of the deeper emotion I was talking about was Rowan's?

"What do you know about Empaths?" I asked Rowan with curious eyes. His face pulled into a frown, his mood changing instantly. Damn, I was ruining it. Killing the mood with a simple question.

"I know a few things. Why do you ask?" His voice was as tight as his face, his eyes searching mine fervently. I smiled at him, releasing a little laugh to try and calm my newly sprung nerves. Looking at his fingers in mine, I twitched my pinky across his palm fondly before continuing.

"It's probably nothing, but Scott said that I'm an Empath. He figured it out when—"

Rowan released my hands and rose, taking a step back. My heart jumped into my throat as I watched his face turn from confusion into revulsion, hatred even. My heart sank as I moved to reconnect with him, to explain I didn't even know what it meant to be what I was. Rowan watched me carefully, taking an additional calculated step away when I took one toward him. *Ouch.*

Chapter Twenty-Two

Rowan

A FUCKING EMPATH! HOW DID I NOT RECOGNIZE IT, THE AURA that was now clear as day to me? It seeped from her, like fog being chased by the morning sun. How had I been so careless? Did she know what I was? Knowledge like that could get me overthrown, it could get me abolished and thrown to the hounds. One Empath in the kingdom was dangerous, but two...*Fuck.*

Eden's eyelids were becoming pink, I could see that she was holding back tears while I treated her like a plague. I questioned how much of it was real. Was she making me feel remorseful? Forcing me to desire running to her, to sweep her into my arms and promising that everything would be alright? A mass was rising in my throat, one of guilt. Shaking my head, I knew that I needed to get out of the room as quickly as possible before caving in to her anguish.

I hastened through the doorway, slamming it behind me and ordering Azrael to keep her on lockdown. Sharp stabs of grief buried themselves in my gut as I walked the corridors, hearing her

fist thumping against the door as I walked. If she was faking inno-
cence, it could be dangerous for someone like me. Knowledge
holds power, and I couldn't risk another second with her in case
she knew exactly what she was. Undoubtedly, she had been sent
by the Coven to destroy me.

I traveled out of the keep and into my favorite of the clus-
tered gardens. It was a small, peaceful place that I could have to
myself whenever I wished. None of the staff would bother me
here. Anchoring myself on the stone bench in front of the fountain, I tried to sort through my scattered thoughts, attempting to
decide on a plan of action.

I couldn't return to her. Not yet. If she failed the Final Trial,
she would be on her way homeward, to forget everything. Being
stripped of her status would exhaust her powers, the mortal realm
would as well, and Empaths didn't exist in the Mortal Realm like
they did in mine. If she succeeded, however, I would be obliged to
figure out how to hide what we were from the council, as well as
the people. History didn't speak warmly of Empaths, particularly
not those who became lovers. *Danger.*

I couldn't handle thinking what my kind would do to us if we
were found out. What they would do to *her.* I shuddered at the
idea. For hours that I didn't bother to count, I sat in the garden
thinking until I felt Eden's energy dim. She had fallen asleep, but
I kept a link attached to her just so that I could be sure that she
was alright, for I had sensed every tear that had fallen from her
eyes from the moment I left.

It was killing me inside to have to be the monstrosity she had
convinced herself that I wasn't. But, it was for her own well-being.
I wanted her. As someone who grew up privileged by royal blood,
I hadn't wanted or needed much in my life. This was different. I
felt connected to Eden. On such a profoundly deep level that it
scared me, and I was not one to be scared easily. I'd seen things,
during battle, that would make grown men weep. Empath's had

that impact on one another. Destined to find their match, they would go to great lengths to protect each other.

For someone in my position, that could be a very dangerous path. All I knew was, despite my fear, I needed her in my life. In one form or another, I couldn't let her go. And, if I had to, it might drive me to insanity.

Chapter Twenty-Three

EVERYTHING FELT STRANGE THE NEXT MORNING. I AWOKE IN Rowan's bed at daybreak, but without him alongside me. He had not returned the previous night. I knew that I must have said something extremely offensive to make him react in such a way. I'd worked out that being an empath must be worse than just being a Witch to the people here. Determining that I'd cried enough the night before, I left the mattress to resume pounding on the door.

"Hello!" I shouted in a croaking, raw voice. My fists beat against the door in bursts of three, disregarding the pain it produced. The night before, I had done this so many times that my hands had curled up in agony, refusing to open from the discomfort that followed after hours of abuse. "I need fresh clothes. And some coffee would be nice!"

The door swung open, and I took three swift steps back. My heart sank when I realized it wasn't Rowan returning to me. Instead, the person that stood in the doorway was Ellie. My spirit warmed slightly at the face of the tiny--whatever she was.

"Morning mistress. Apologies for the tardiness, I wasn't aware that you had been transferred." She wheeled in my breakfast and a change of clothes. The heap of attire seemed much larger than usual that morning. Ellie grunted as she hoisted it onto the bed while I poured myself a cup of coffee and sat down, hungry, and ready for the day to be over with already.

I watched her in curiosity. "Forgive me, El, I'm in the habit of saying things I'm not supposed to lately, so forgive me if I come off as offensive by asking, but...What are you, exactly?"

Ellie chuckled, laying out the breakfast feast and wiping her hands clean against her apron.

"I don't think that's inappropriate at all, mistress. I am a Brownie. Proud of the fact too!" She shot me a toothy grin and moved around me to start pinning my hair into a low bun that sat tight against my nape. With her behind me, I ate the rest of my breakfast in silence, drinking the coffee until the pot was empty. Pondering what had happened between Rowan and me, hoping that there was a way to fix it. Ellie bowed to me once she had finished grooming my hair into a stylish, military look.

"Good luck at the coliseum today mistress, I'm running late for my other chores, and am sorry to say that I can't help you to dress this morning. It is my hope that, when we next meet, I will be calling you 'Your Grace.'" She gave me one last hopeful smile, which I returned before she left, permitting me to examine my latest gear.

Coliseum, a place where hundreds of people watch you battle to the death? I tried to push away the idea of today's Trial possibly holding an audience, a detail that nobody had mentioned. Not that I was told much of anything; it wasn't new. I picked up the first piece of new clothing to examine it.

The flawlessly cut virescent scales layered over one another and mimicked those of the Dragon that I had encountered in the cave. But these were smaller, finer and had been polished to a gleam. The sleeves were long and clung to my arms with surprising elasticity. Scales across the breast jingled as I pulled the top on. The fit of it was perfect, this outfit had been made for my body, down to the last curve. I tugged on the plain leggings afterward, as well as the pieces of metal meant to protect my thighs and shoulders.

It was tricky, buckling the leather straps on my own. But after an hour or so, I was completely outfitted in the armor. I realized soon after that I should have put my boots on before all the heavy shit, but it was too late. Cursing at myself for it, I spent the next twenty minutes doing just that. A chunk of hair had loosened from the bun on the back of my head during the struggle and rested between my eyes as I sat up. Blowing it away before it got stuck in the sweat that was now beading my forehead, I stood again, heading for the door.

Azrael was in the hall waiting for me, something I discovered after turning the handle of the door, surprised it opened at that time. He looked me up and down disapprovingly before advancing to jerk on the pieces of armor that I had misplaced on my shoulders. I felt like an insignificant little ant under his judgmental stare.

"So, um, where am I supposed to go for this event?" I asked softly.

"I'll be accompanying you to the coliseum. Lord Blaive awaits you there." He said shortly.

"Yeah, I'm sure he does," I mumbled, remembering the fit he had thrown the night before when he had left me without so much as an explanation. Azrael's wide nostrils flared, his pitch-black brows angry with lines setting between them. He was Fae, so getting those wrinkles must not have been an easy task to accomplish. Pulling me up the hall, he waited to speak again until we were out of earshot of the other guards.

"You don't understand, do you? Stupid Witch, stupid mortal." He growled and stared at me like I had just kicked his dog. "The

Lord favors you. So much, that he was willing to reveal knowledge to you that could get him overthrown. Are you a moron?" He jabbed a humongous finger into my temple. "Because right now, in this moment, you look like a damn fool, woman."

"I—what? I—" It was challenging to find the words to respond. With a deep breath, I decided that my best course of action would be to show him that I, too, had feelings. "I told him something about myself, and he ran away from me. I've done nothing wrong here! Other than to be what I was born as. What is his excuse?"

"You don't know him. The boy would have been killed by his father, like Fenris and his kind were," His eyes softened just slightly. "But the young lord survived. Because Alara, his mother, and yours worked together to stifle the boy's powers. When they were discovered, Rowan's father thought the worst. He never found out about Rowan being an empath. The boy lived because of your mother's sacrifice, Eden. Do you understand that? Rowan knows of this. But, he—" Azrael's head snapped ahead, hearing the footsteps long before I did. He looked back at me and leaned in.

"Win the Trial. Earn his trust and respect. Then talk to him like a grownup, little girl."

"Wait, back up. Who is Fenris?"

"Your father," He whispered, shaking his head to cut off any other questions. Ah, so my biological father had a name. It wasn't much to go on, but I'd take it. The news of my mother's sacrifice struck a chord in me. It was a hard thing to find out that my mother hadn't deserted me just to run to la-la-land for a different life. Guilt was what I was feeling. Shame for hating her.

With that, Azrael was back to being a bodyguard, leading into the courtyard that was filled to the max with crowds of people. The mob exploded into a roar when they saw my face. Not one of anger, but excitement. It was unbelievable. I felt like I finally knew what it was like to be famous. How did I even have fans?

"They watch through the crystal balls," Azrael whispered, as though he read my mind. Well, now I just felt embarrassed. People had watched me in each Trial, including the part where I almost died at the hands of---well---myself. Fingers reached out to me from every direction, trying to touch whatever they could land on as the screaming grew louder with encouraging cries. I smiled meekly and waved to as many people as I could while we passed through, headed toward the city below.

The enormous entrance to the city was hanging open, enabling the townspeople to approach the keep freely. Under the vigilant eyes of the guards, of course. I even saw one guy as he tried to make a run for it through the castle entrance. He was immediately pounced on and stopped before he could lay a finger on the building. *Sheesh, these people take things pretty seriously around here.*

A short walk later, we strolled upon the main street of the town that I still didn't know the name of. It was my first time in the city while people were awake and the streets were bustling. The sound of children's merriment filled the crisp morning air, along with the parents screaming at them to get their chores done instead of gaping at the contestant walking the dusty, cobblestone path. Merchants were also a prominent source of the commotion, bellowing out their goods in hopes that the new parade of bodies would be tempted enough to stop in for some skewered lamb, fresh fish just pulled from the sea, or a nice beaded necklace.

It almost felt homey, with the flourishing lives of the people there. The atmosphere made me feel whole with a sense of deliverance from the solitude the castle had cast upon me over the past several days. Not all of the faces were happy to see me, however. I saw many of them twisted in distaste as I passed by. Deciding not to let them get to me, I set my sights on a small child stretching and arm out for me. She was perhaps four or five and clutching something in her pudgy fist while hopping up and down on the dirt. I glanced at Azrael before stopping to kneel in front of the girl.

"Princess Eden!" She giggled nervously, stretching her other fist of fingers to her mouth so that she could chew on one for comfort. I smiled at her warmly, nodding to her still-outstretched arm.

"What do you have there?" I asked gently.

"I made it for you, my momma told me that I could." I peered into her doe-eyes of gray, noting that even Fae babes were beautiful. Opening my palm beneath her hand, I allowed her to drop the ball of mud and sticks into it. Trying not to let the disgust show on my face, I gave her a grin and thanked her for what I'm sure she had carefully constructed just for me. The mother of the girl rushed to her child, apologizing for the little one's boldness. She moved so quickly that her tattered skirt nearly enveloped the girl completely, before hurrying her elsewhere.

"Beat that mean woman today, Princess!" The little girl called, trying to wriggle free of her mother's grasp. I waved to her and took my place at Azrael's side again, disregarding the perplexed stare he gave me. The structure of sticky mud was still in my hand. He glanced down at it and raised an eyebrow.

"Are you going to keep that horse shit in your hand all the way to the coliseum?" He grumbled.

"Ew," I said, slinging it to the ground, hoping the little girl couldn't see as I discarded her gift. Azrael removed a stained fabric from the inside of his suit of armor, handing it over to me. I happily accepted and cleaned my hand before moving to hand it back. His eyes traveled from the cloth and back up to me.

"You may keep it."

Not that I didn't appreciate it, I smiled at him and tossed the cloth into the crowd, watching for a moment as a group of people shoved each other aside to grab at it. Grimacing, I prayed that they would at least clean the thing before including it in their household washcloths.

"We must maintain our route, Lady Eden," Azrael said, using my proper title for the first time. It felt strange. Like I was a little girl playing dress-up and everyone else was being forced to play along. I tried not to think about it much as let my gaze wander, searching for the coliseum. It wasn't long before the enormous building was unveiled, behind stacks of impeccably constructed dwellings and taverns. My mouth hung slightly ajar as I observed the long lines of people waiting to get in.

Despite the bickering amongst them, the ambiance felt charged and ample with feel-good energy. These people were ready for whatever the day had in store for me. Who knew how long they had been waiting for an event such as this to occur? I wondered, with a jolt of fear, if the protection spells would hold up this time. Also, how many of these people were here to see me fail. Azrael used his authority and brute force to get us past the thousands idling outside of the coliseum.

Once indoors, when the door had slammed shut, the air shifted, becoming oddly tranquil. A part of me longed to run back outside, to become a part of the masses rather than a contestant. I hadn't felt much in the way of nerves while walking. But being in that silence sent it barreling through me all at once. My feet halted in place, and I slapped a hand onto Azrael's shoulder to keep myself from toppling over and losing my breakfast.

He rolled his eyes and heaved a sigh, allowing me to take my time managing myself. Once I was sure that I could stand straight again, I nodded at him, letting him lead us where we needed to be. Being so wrapped up in the thought of people watching me in this event, I hadn't given much thought to the location. What I knew about the coliseum in ancient Rome was that it had been used for battling gladiators.

Today would be a fight, I was sure of it, observing the massive amphitheater. Seats were not yet filling, but I acknowledged that that would be soon. Terror was gripping my gut with claw-like daggers. My footsteps echoed with the clinking of my armor as we walked the outskirts of the structure. Looking up, I could see a velarium high above, shutting out the sun's bright rays so that the entire structure retained a cryptic feel.

With a peek over the edge, I was able to see the arena floor several hundred feet below. There sat a labyrinth of erected stones at the bottom. I started to squint my eyes for a better look but Azrael was quick to snatch me away from the edge, giving me a disapproving scowl like he had when fixing my armor.

"No scheming." He grumbled, shoving me to the other side of him so that I wouldn't get another opportunity to look at the base level. Groaning, I released the temptation to shove him over the side and marched beside him submissively. His steps were growing swift, more urgent, as we neared the corridor that led to the room I'd be held in. He gave the room a scan, as though he expected someone to jump out wielding a blade at any moment.

"I have been ordered to stay by you until the Trial begins; however, I'm afraid I have more pressing matters to attend to with his Grace." He motioned me into the room, deciding that nobody was waiting to kill me inside. Soon after, a woman stepped in who was cloaked head to toe in pearly-white robes. Her head was lowered. Azrael nodded to her and then to me before returning to the entrance.

"Best of luck to you, Lady Eden." He said and closed the door. I shifted on my feet awkwardly as the woman began to circle me, her fingers outstretched. I could sense the tingling of magic on my skin as she worked. Her appearance was familiar to me, which I soon pinpointed. She had been one of the women with the crystal balls in the first Trial. Or she resembled them, I couldn't be sure that she was the same.

"What are you doing?" I asked her, twisting in an attempt to examine her face as she passed in front of me for the third time. Her hands and feet kept moving, though she granted me a flash of her gleaming violet eyes beneath the cowl. Perhaps she wasn't used to being spoken to directly, or maybe I was messing with her concentration. Either way, I was somewhat taken aback when she responded.

"Protection." She whispered, her voice like that of a serpent as it slithered from her tongue and pierced my ears. I shivered at the sound, despite my trying hard not to. Her full, dark lips curled into a smirk. I wondered if she enjoyed watching people react to her disturbing speech, and figured she probably did, being as how she kept that eerie smile on her face right up until the last round of the spell. *Weird.*

"Is this spell different from before?" I asked her. She gave me a nod.

"Stronger." She said simply. I'd never get used to that voice. I wished she would just shut up so that I wouldn't feel so frightened under her stare. "Close your eyes."

I did as she asked, ignoring my brain telling me to disobey just so that I could keep my eyes on her. She was quick and silent in her steps, which had me questioning whether she was moving at all. My eyes popped back open at the feeling of something heavy being clasped around each of my wrists, confirming that she had moved, and in doing so grabbed the chains from the walls.

"Shackles!" I cried out. "I'm in a prison cell, which I'm certain will be bolted when you leave. Do you really think I'm going anywhere?"

She didn't speak another word, just spun on her heel and exited the room, leaving me in the middle of the floor attached to the walls with the rusty old chains. A grate in the tall ceiling above provided fragments of sunshine that cast bands of light across my face and arms. I waited there, dropping to my knees for a touch of comfort while I listened to the voices of people beginning to gush into the stands beyond my cell walls. The sound of it had my heart hammering inside my chest.

Nervous sweat trickled down my temples the longer I kneeled there, my body was growing hypersensitive due to the adrenaline pumping through my veins. After an unknown amount of time had passed, an unexpected tremor jolted the floor, causing me to wind my fingers around the chains and pull against them tightly to keep myself from falling over. The grinding of stone against stone scraped my eardrums as the chamber began to descend like a giant elevator. I breathed heavily as I watched the door and its wall lift higher and higher. The other three walls stayed firmly in place as I worked to get to my feet as gracefully as possible in preparation for whatever lay at the bottom. It was a slow process getting there, and my legs were aching by the end of it from using every muscle that I owned to remain standing.

Finally, after what seemed like hours, the room came to a halt, and the wall where the door had been was now open to the arena's base level. The sunlight that I had been graced with before was now long gone, so far above me that I could only just make out a speck of the golden shine. Peering toward the arena, I could discern torches burning heartily against the stone slabs which looked a hundred times larger at eye level than they had from above.

"Welcome visitors from far and wide!" Rowan's voice thundered throughout the entire stadium so powerfully that I stumbled backward. Wanting to see his face, if even for a moment, I searched the bits of the stands that I could see from inside of the room. Thousands of people were up above, and I was provided no such luck. "Today, we will witness the Trial of Might as a unified set of Kingdoms!" The crowd went wild, screaming joyfully in response to his words.

"Most of you have watched these women while they earned their places in this prestigious battle. Today, you will behold the birth of a new Fae Queen!" His voice was strong, entrusting, and robust. The assemblage loved it. I realized that I loved it too, forgetting momentarily that I was still pissed about him taking off on me. The way he spoke was inspirational, motivating even. Like he wasn't just explaining the Trial, but a part of it this time. "My finest warriors have captured a creature from the far southern countries. They hunted the beast for nearly a year to track it down and return it here to be unleashed in the arena--" As he spoke my shackles snapped open, permitting me to rub my wrists and start walking forward, into the arena's rugged terrain.

The roars from the crowd became deafening as I moved out of the shadows and into the torchlight. From the way that people in all directions were screaming, drowning out Rowan's voice, I could only assume that the additional two contestants had been set free as well. It took a long while for the uproar to settle down enough for the Prince to continue. I'd be lying if I said it didn't feel damn great to experience that type of support.

"Yes! Show your love for your heroines!" Rowan had a smile on his lips, I could hear it in his voice. It made me wonder if he was somewhere up there, gazing down at me. My stomach flipped, and I began to scan the crowd again. "As I was saying, everyone, please also give our Manticore welcome applause."

The crowd went absolutely insane. This time it wasn't all happy and cheering, though. The screams of women sounded all around me, along with the combined gasps of random people. I swallowed hard. Knowing that this couldn't be a good indication, I searched my mind, trying to remember what exactly a Manticore was. A guttural cry came from within the rock formations and sent a chill through my bones. It sounded like a wild cat, but larger, more powerful. I wanted to run but stood firmly in place with bulging eyes and twitching fingers.

"The champions will need to fend off the Manticore whilst attempting to best each other. Furthermore, there may be more surprises in store for them. Defenses are fastened to the inner chamber's walls, where the monster roams. Do you hear me, contestants?" My eyes flicked back down to the structure, every muscle in my body tensing as I started to run like hell into it. My breathing was shallow with fear as I entered the walls, carefully making my way along the side with my eyes peeled, watching for movement.

"There is only one rule. You may not kill each other-" A little bit of booing sounded from the crowd. Apparently, they wanted to watch us die. *Too bad for them*, I thanked the stars. "When your opponent has been bested, and can no longer fight back, you must cease and allow them to shimmer away. Without further ado, let the Trial begin!"

With that, it was like a sound barrier came up between the crowd and us. Everything fell eerily silent, only just faint muffled voices came from far off. It was like listening to music at the lowest volume, the noise was there, but I couldn't hear much of anything apart from the crackling torches. I bent my neck to look overhead as the sound of flapping wings passed above my hiding place.

Compressing myself into the wall, I did what I could to hide from view as Sephial soared through the air. Another set of wings blasted a loose curl from behind my ear and sent it swirling around my face as the Harpy screeched in rage. I observed in loathing as I realized that the additional wings were those belonging to Nija. *Of course, she has wings, why not?* Exactly as Sephial had figured out which direction she was coming from, Nija raked a clawed hand across her face. Sephial spun out of control, free-falling downward, only just able to regain her control before crashing into a stone slab. She twisted and gave a great push with her wings, grabbing hold of Nija's ankles. The two plunged from the air, entwined with each other until they had fallen behind the stone walls and out of sight.

Determining that this would be the ideal moment to arm myself with something other than my untamed spells, I un-plastered myself from the wall and sprang into a run. Coming upon stone walls repeatedly, I was growing discouraged in realizing that I might never find the heart of the maze. Taking a left, then a right, then an additional two rights, the walls began to swirl around me, dizzying me to the point of nausea. I clasped my face in my hands and shook my head fervently, attempting to rid myself of the confusion heavy in my mind.

"What's the matter, little one, are you lost?" I jerked my face up to meet Nija's gleaming stare. What the hell had happened to her being preoccupied with Sephial? I checked my wrist to make sure that she hadn't been defeated. Seeing that no point had been branded there, I looked to Nija in confusion. "I have bigger fish to fry," the Demon chuckled.

Chapter Twenty-Four

Mustering all of my strength through that fuzziness in my brain, I aimed a row of fingers at her, hurling the smallest flash of electricity zipping in her direction. She coolly watched as it flew past her and into a wall that was several feet from where she stood. She dropped her head with a wicked smile, preparing her wings behind her as she opened her clawed hands in an attack stance.

"Weak and pathetic. Just like dear mommy was when my family convinced King Blaive to cut her down like the weed she was," she said, making my jaw grow tight and my arm muscles harden. So it was *her* who had been the cause of my mother's death. But how? How did she get under the King's skin enough to make him murder his own wife alongside my mother in cold blood? Nija watched me carefully, edging closer as I raised a second hand between us, my lip curled into a snarl. "What's the matter? Did I strike a nerve?" she asked sweetly.

With added power surging up inside of me, I hurled another thunderbolt at her. This one connected, but only hard enough to push one of her shoulders backward and piss her off. She peered at the smoke curling down the length of her arm and then back at me, her eyes narrowing so that they were only slits of scarlet light.

"We would have let her live, you know. Had she taken our side in the war. With the power of the Coven supporting us, we could have put an end to it once and for all. Especially since the fool of a King rid us of our Empaths."

So there it was. Empaths were evil too. Great, I had a lot of things working against me just because I existed. I was beginning to understand Rowan's reaction, though.

"It doesn't appear to me that you want the war to end, Nija. You seem perfectly content in the chaos you generate. People are dying, your own included. Does that mean nothing to you?"

"I don't worry about the lives that have been lost, fool. Those of Rowan's maternal family included." She snarled. "I care about commanding the seven Kingdoms. Primarily this one."

I dodged as she elevated into the air and spiraled toward me. It wasn't quick enough to evade a slashing of nails across my cheek that flung me onto my ass. I disregarded the stinging blood on my face and scrambled to my feet, followed by a sprint that took me several feet away from Nija. She whirled around, wings still beating to keep her airborne. Opening her mouth as if to speak, she paused and cocked her head to listen for something that I couldn't detect.

Before I could question her further, Sephial crashed into her from behind, taking both of them to the stony ground. Sephial held Nija against the stone with a taloned foot to the chest. All it would take is one hard push with that massive claw that was readied above the demon's heart. Sephial was eager to finish it but was hindered by a grinding that vibrated through the ground beneath us. Another noise rose into the air as well, something other than the harsh scraping of stone.

"Water?" I asked no one in particular. Sephial's vivid eyes grew, and her hold on Nija slackened as she prepared herself for flight. It was just enough for the Demon to send a sharp elbow into the back of her knee. My hand flew over my open mouth as Nija brought her to her knees, swinging a fist across the Harpy's face before pivoting her to the ground. Nija's eyes snapped in my direction while she held her forearm across the other female's neck. The look was one that told me she would deal with me later. I swallowed and began to back up. With a look to my left, I spotted the next passage and bolted. I wanted to put as much space between myself and that crazy bitch as I could.

The roaring of water was growing closer. It continued to expand the further I ran until it was all I could hear. Stopping for just a second to take a breather, I looked up just in time to view a gigantic wave before it came crashing down into the labyrinth. My feet were swept from beneath me right before my body was slammed into the stone wall by the sheer strength of the tide. My arms stroked against the current wildly, trying to find their way to the surface. The liquid was dim and murky and I soon understood that searching for something to grab onto was hopeless. The strength of the current didn't allow me to do much of anything. I could only submit to being washed away like a petal in a stream.

My lungs began squeezing in my chest, howling for the sweet flavor of oxygen as the racing water hurled me in every direction, including straight into hard stone. Just before I thought that I was going to lose consciousness, my head breached the surface. Wheezing to draw in as much air as I could, I forced my eyes open and took in my surroundings with wild panic. I was being pushed through a crude, topless hallway and directly into the core of the maze.

I knew it to be the center because of the wide-open area, and the soft glisten of weapons skirting the walls. It spilled into the opening, depositing me in the middle of the room as the turbulent river slowed into two feet of dingy, standing water. Trying to regain my footing, I slipped, sending myself face-first beneath the dark, glassy surface. Quickly, I shoved my hands onto the floor to push against it, making another effort to stand.

The second time, I succeeded in getting to my feet and allowed my breathing to regulate before venturing to the wall of weaponry. Understanding completely that I had no idea how to use any of them, I supposed they would give me a tiny bit more protection against the others. Gazing across the array, my sights settled on a gleaming silver short sword with a simplistic, leather-bound hilt. Water sloshed around my knees as I made my way to the underside of the weapon and reached a hand up to extract it from the chain.

As soon as my fingers had encircled the handle, a fiery breeze, brought by the vibration of a menacing snarl, warmed my freezing, water-soaked back. The hair at my nape prickled, standing straight up as I slowly rotated my head to gaze over my shoulder. The water rippled around a shadowy mass that stood in the center of the room where I had been only minutes before. Hypnotizing bronze eyes stared directly at me. The shining spheres seemed to glow in the light of the few torches that hadn't been snuffed out by the waves.

A shiver traveled down my backbone as I followed the creature with my eyes. It lowered into a crouch. With a single step, the beast moved closer, sending a fresh wave of water lapping up my thigh. This had to be the Manticore Rowan had spoken of. The thing had moved into the light, unveiling the tawny face of a large cat. Its mighty fringe was matted with filth and wet. Scars riddled its disfigured face that was now pulled into an angry snarl. My breath hitched in my chest as it took another step closer.

Shredded wings that resembled bats were partially unfolded on the creature's back, allowing enough space between them for me to see an enormous tailpiece of a scorpion. My blood went cold as I realized it was aimed at me. With a jerk of the sword, it came tumbling into my palm, and I spun to face the animal before it could fill my body with venom. A clicking growl spilled from the thing's throat, sending a chill up my spine. Screaming internally, I reminded myself to pull it together and think of a plan.

Deciding that there was no way that I would be able to take that thing down with the sword, I knew that I'd have to resort to my powers. Amidst a cautious downward glance, while taking a slow step sideways, an idea came to mind. If I could get to higher ground, I could give this cat a shock that it might not be able to walk away from. Scanning the room as quickly as possible, I saw that there were protruding ledges on the walls that were wide enough to place my feet on.

"You're wet too, idiot." I snapped at myself while edging my way to the closest one. Placing my feet on it, I moved carefully as not to disturb the animal while wobbling and trying to keep my balance. It seemed ready to attack with its yellowing-teeth bared in a fury. I knew that if I sent out a bolt of lightning, I might be signing my own death contract as well as his.

I can't produce electricity right now, but I might be able to manipulate the water to send this fucker as far away from me as possible. I began to rotate my fingers after dropping the sword onto the ledge behind my feet. Pulling the energy that I had somewhat learned to harness into my chest, I shifted it into my outstretched fingers. Ripples, the size of my arms began to form, darting out from my perch. "Yes! Do you want to go for a swim kitty cat?"

The pupils of the monster dilated and its hind legs shifted into a position that would allow it to close the gap between us, ripping me to shreds in the process. I needed to do something and fast. My eyebrows drew together in concentration as I brought every emotion that I could to the surface, particularly what I felt about what Nija had revealed while trying to kill me. The water below started to swirl around the circular space, a gentle whirlpool dragging at the Manticore's tan fur.

With a wide swoop of my hand, I succeeded in hastening the momentum of my current and flipping the creature onto its side. I strained forward to make a larger sweeping movement through the air, observing cautiously as the thing clawed at the water, trying to regain its footing. The whirling water below rose in level as I worked, sloshing against my boots, the faster that the current passed. With a decisive push, I hurled my hands forward, catching myself just before tipping into the dangerous pool. My feet held fast as I continued forming a wave that consumed one-fourth of the water from my side of the chamber. My wrist was stinging, indicating the downfall of another contestant, but I knew that I couldn't focus on that.

With another push, I drove the wave away from me. My hands trembled at the weight of the spell as my tide consumed the giant cat and drove it up and over at least three walls. It wasn't much, but I wasn't in the same room as that thing anymore. With a tilt of my head, I strained my ears over the splashes of water that had begun settling back into place. The Manticore was bellowing, offering me some hope that its pitiful wings wouldn't be enough to lift it into the air and back to me.

Jumping down into the water that was swelling back into that side of the room, I froze as the sound of my worst fear fluttered overhead.

Chapter Twenty-Five

I JERKED MY FACE UP TO SEE NIJA NOSE-DIVING AT ME.

She slammed me into the ground with such force that I felt my head bounce off of the stone beneath the water. I gasped and clapped a hand around her wrist as she brought me back up with surprising strength. Thinking swiftly, I slid the blade in my other hand across the top of her forearms.

Nija shrieked and yanked her hands up to her temples, permitting me to scramble to my feet and prepare a spell. Our faces illuminated with soft, orange light as the flames swept across my knuckles. Nija looked more monstrous than ever, licking the blood from her arms with a forked tongue before smiling at me and tucking her wings against her back.

"I'm going to kill you, Witch. Just like I killed your little Siren friend."

"You?" I said, pausing mid-step. My face revealed the horror I felt, which made Nija's smile widen. Not that I was surprised that she had done it, but because she was openly admitting to it. I wondered if the sound barrier worked both ways or if the crowd had heard her confession. When nobody came to collect her, I settled on my first thought.

"Yes, I couldn't let her run off and expose what I had done." She ran at me, easily knocking the sword from my hand and wrapping her fist around my throat. My powers were weakened from the wave, she sensed it, and her grip tightened to the point that I couldn't breathe anymore. I retrieved the memory of my first time using spells against a Demon. Upon pushing my flaming hand onto her face, Nija only threw her head back and released a sinister cackle.

"Stupid witch," She snickered and glared into my eyes. "I'm a Demon, born of fire--"

I shifted the power to a burst of lightning, giving both of us a good zap that blew us apart. It hadn't been the best idea, but it was the only thing that I could come up with. The electric shock wasn't strong enough to carry through the water, thankfully, or we would have both been dead. I climbed to my feet, my chest heaving and skin tingling while Nija did the same. She cleaned a line of blood from her nose and crinkled it at me in a fury.

"You're running out of energy, witch. And I will gladly pull the life from your weakened body. When I'm finished with you, I will take the Prince as my husband. He will make a nice puppet. Just as his pathetic father was to my own kind."

"The only pathetic one here, Nija," I gasped between words, feeling my knees shake as they threatened to give out entirely, "is you. Why not just let things be? End the war and become powerful that way. Why do you have to be so destructive?"

With another lunge she was upon me, holding me in the air as she thrust her wings to lift the two of us high above the ground. I had no weapon and no energy left to fight back. The best I could do was bare my teeth and try to rip her hands from my throat with my nails. It didn't help, Nija held tight, hovering above the structure with me at her mercy. Her lips moved close to mine and she blew out a thick, indigo mist, sending a tingle across my flesh. I felt the protection spell waver and crumble off of my body.

"I want what the rest of my people do. To snuff out the

revolting Seelie Court." Her pointed teeth flashed, every word falling from her lips dripping with venom. "They are a blemish on this Realm, one that has held power for far too long. They pushed my people into the Demonlands so that we didn't spoil their pure world. Your Coven could have followed us, but your stupid mother wouldn't give in. So, you and your kind are enemies in the eyes of my people. And they will all die, just as you are about to."

She released her grip, allowing me to slip from her wet fingers and fall through the air. My back slapped against the water, and Nija was close behind. Just as I sank below the surface, she placed a boot at my throat to make sure that I stayed there. Fighting against her strength, I began to feel completely dejected as water flooded into my lungs and ears. My sight grew darker as my mind started to become hazy. Death was upon me. I could feel it breathing down my neck.

My body went slack and I gave in to my fate as Nija shoved her boot even harder against my throat. I had expended all of my energy. There was nothing left to pull from. Flashes of my father's eyes crossed my mind. Ava and her infectious smile. I was at peace, with them there to guide me. Memories flooded into me, and I felt like I was floating, the weight of Nija's foot no longer pressing me down. My mind didn't register that I actually *was* floating and the strong hands as they pulled me from the water. Sounds of roaring applause were barely audible over the pounding in my ears. Something heavy slammed into my back, forcing some of the water from my lungs and out of my mouth and nose.

"*Breathe, Eden!*" Rowan shouted, but his voice in my ears was only a dull murmur. Another slam to the back forced even more water to get expelled from my lungs, allowing me to take in a deep gulp of air. The entire world was spinning. I couldn't force my blurred vision to focus on anything, and my legs were too weak to hold me. Panic set in, forcing a familiar trickle of power to bleed through me. Just as it did, everything started to come into focus. I could make out Rowan's face, tight with worry, and Nija struggling to recover after being thrown into a wall.

Rowan exhaled an immense sigh of relief as I regarded the water at my feet that began diminishing. He picked me up and set me against a wall before turning back to Nija, his hand in the air, forcing her to her knees. I watched as he brought his hand into a tight fist and she crumpled to the floor before shimmering away. A burning on my wrist told me that she had been defeated as if the image of it hadn't shown already. Rowan hurried back to me, lifting me in his powerful arms.

I couldn't resist the heaviness in my eyelids and body any longer and gave into the darkness as the spectators erupted into chaos.

When I came to, Rowan was standing over me. His face had never looked more beautiful nor frightened. I sat up suddenly, feeling amazingly intact. His eyes grew as I grinned at him.

"Did I win, or did you?" I croaked. Apparently, healing didn't save me from getting a sore throat. It probably came from that disgusting water. Who knows what was in it? Rowan pulled me into a tight embrace, and I relished in the warmth of his body, feeling more comfortable than I ever had in my life.

"You did, Eden." He said with a laugh in his voice. "Nija was going to kill you, I had to step in. I'm so sorry. We were unaware that she could dispel the protection charms. You nearly drowned..."

"I'm alright," I said and felt a little disappointed when his grip fell loose and he drew his arms back to his sides. I noticed that I was in his room again, this time, not without an audience. With a glance down, I was relieved to see that, this time, I wasn't naked. Though, I wasn't in the armor any longer either. It had been replaced with a pale, moon-colored shirt that fell to my thighs. One of *his*, I realized with a blush.

"Can we speak, alone?" I asked Rowan, giving him a sideways glance. He nodded and shooed the group of women away, most of whom I'd never seen before. Once he had returned to my side, I could see the sadness and something more in his eyes.

"We won't have long." He said and sat beside me on the bed, twisting his torso so that he was facing me.

"Rowan..." I paused, working to think of what to say to him. He used the silence to speak for himself. Taking one of my hands, he placed something in it and curled his fingers around mine. Continuing to hold my hand, he looked into my eyes, the twinge of that extra something still lying deep within his.

"Eden, I think that you should return home. Take care of your sister and your father. The healing that you exhibited after your fight with Nija was nothing short of remarkable. My own healers don't possess the kind of power that you used to mend your body. It should be sufficient in aiding your father's health."

"You want me to leave?" I said in disbelief, ignoring what he had just said about healing myself. I wanted to shake him, to force him to reveal whatever it was that he was hiding. His gaze lowered to my hand as his thumb swept across it in a comforting caress. "But, I won, doesn't that mean--"

"The wedding is set for midday tomorrow. I am giving you an out, Eden. Take it. Return to your loved ones. You will be safe there. Nija is back with her people, but...I broke our contract and she wants you dead."

"So, you are sending me away, just like that?" I jerked my hand from his and scooted to the opposite side of the bed. Rocking my head in utter disbelief, I stared through the tall glass of the windows at the darkened sky that had become littered with stars. I'd never taken the time to admire the beauty of this place, and I felt like I would never have the opportunity again. "Is it because I told you that I'm an Empath?"

"Yes," Rowan answered after a few minutes of thinking on it. My heart squeezed in my chest.

"Guess what happened between us was just--" hot tears rolled down my cheeks as the words crossed through my mind and rolled off of my tongue, "a transaction. Like what you had with Nija."

"Not in the least," Rowan pushed himself behind me, wrapping his arms around my waist as he placed a soft kiss upon my shoulder and pressed his forehead onto my temple. My body wanted to relax into him, to feel what I felt for him the night before. It all seemed so far away, but I wanted him to pull my arms above my head, to rip my clothes off with his teeth, and to give me all of himself. However, that wasn't reality. The truth was that he was throwing me away for something that was out of my understanding or control.

"I'll go," I whispered, pushing the sobs threatening my voice away. Rowan's arms tightened for a few blissful seconds. I drew in a long breath through my nose, inhaling his lush, woody aroma. It sent a new flood of tears dispersing across my face and onto my chest. A thumb swept across the stream softly, clearing the sorrow from my face. Permitting my head to fall into Rowan's palm, I wanted to stay there with him, to keep us in that moment forever.

"Thank you." He said in a rough voice. I could hear the pain in it. "Eden, I—" He swallowed hard and sighed, his breath warming my nape. "I love you."

I considered responding to him. The words cut deep. Why would he tell me something like that after telling me he didn't want me? Maybe saying something would have changed things. But a bigger part of me told me that it wouldn't, so I lay there in silence, allowing each aching moment to pass between us without a word. How could he love me and not want to fight to keep me? He was right though, either way, I needed to see my family.

"I won't force you to respond, as much as I wish that you would. The word that you searched for the first time you were here was *Brruntek*. It will open the portal."

It was over too soon as he pulled away and stood up, going to the door to allow his people in once again. I repeated the word in my head over and over as the ones around me that I didn't even care to look at chatted about wedding details and my new room. A Fae woman, Elven, by the look of her, pulled me to my feet and hustled me out of the room.

"You shouldn't be with your partner until the wedding night." She smiled pleasantly and led me several doors down to my new room. It looked almost identical to Rowan's but just slightly smaller. Somehow, it was still much bigger than my first room in the castle. Guessing that I had been upgraded due to the Trials being over, I let myself fall into the fluffy bed. The woman tried to prod me for details about my appearance preferences until realizing I wasn't in the mood to talk about it.

As soon as she had taken her leave, I allowed myself to cry until I fell asleep, my arms curled around my legs like the sad child I had been the night of losing my mother.

Chapter Twenty-Six

IT WAS THE MORNING OF MY WEDDING, AND I HAD BEEN outfitted by a foursome of Fae women.

The fluid ivory gown that I had been put into was flawless. My toned shoulders were complemented by the thick straps which were glittering with tiny diamonds that trailed down to my waist, where a long, silver belt hung loosely. The bodice of the dress was tight-fitting, and the skirt fell into a short train behind me. Another long piece of cloth, fastened with a diamond-encrusted clasp at my throat, settled over my shoulders and down the length of the skirt.

My hair had been fluffed and braided into a full heap of crimson that was stuffed with baby's breath and white roses. To top it all off, the women had given me a pair of white heels and a crystal tiara that sat atop my crown. I had decided over my morning coffee what I was going to do, which was not what my future husband had asked. Rowan was going to get me, whether he wanted to or not.

I was sure of my choice to run home, check on my father and sister, tell them everything and then return to be wed. I didn't care about Nija and her associates. I'd willingly stand at Rowan's side and fight them off until the end of time. All I needed was a moment alone. I tried to remember what the time rules were, knowing I wouldn't have much of it when I returned to the Mortal Realm.

Finally, as the last person left my room, I dug under my pillow to find the crystal Rowan had provided me. Using what I could remember of Harper's design, I pulled the crystal through the air and smiled as the shining light hung there, just as it was supposed to. Once I was satisfied with the image, I locked the door and took a deep breath before speaking the word.

"Brruntek."

Much to my amazement, the portal split open. With another glance around, for no reason, because I knew I was alone, I stepped through it. The ride was much smoother than it had been the first time around. Possibly because I embraced the magic surrounding me instead of fighting it as I had before. My shoes slammed into the ground, and with a scan, I knew myself to be somewhere just outside of my home city. Stuffing the crystal safely into the chest piece of my gown, I thought about the bounty hunter and what he had said when we first met. This world mirrored the Fae Realm, and I was probably lucky that I hadn't ended up in the wall of a building or something like that.

The sun had just begun to set on the horizon as I trudged into town, ignoring the stares from people who were probably wondering what I was doing wearing that many gems. I doubted that they could tell their authenticity but, to be safe, I broke into a run. I didn't stop until I had made it to the street where my house sat, my heart thundered with adrenaline and dread. What if Ava decided to hate me endlessly afterward?

I shook my head, knowing that I didn't have a choice. I needed Rowan, and I needed them too. I'd come home and visit with the magical crystals as often as I'd be allowed. Ava would have to understand. She was, after all, the main person in my world urging me to have a love life.

"Well, Ava, you've got it." I murmured as I ascended the steps to my house, gazing at the porch fondly. I would miss it there. My fingers delayed on the door handle as I wanted to take in every piece of this place. To lock it up inside and always have with me. The soft glow coming through the living room window told me that Ava would be just on the other side. Taking a long breath, I twisted the handle and pushed the door open.

Ava's wide, hazel eyes found mine and then moved down the length of my body. My focus fell to her lips, and I realized that something was off. Her mouth had been gagged. A shift alongside her also caught my attention, driving me into a fighting stance. My muscles loosened as I realized the movement had been my father, looking like he was at death's door with the purplish bags under his eyes and a rail-thin body.

"Dad? Ava? What happened?" I hurried over and started to untie my father first, reaching over just long enough to pull the cloth from Ava's lips. I did the same with my father. He didn't look well at all, with his hair that had mostly gone gray hanging past his ears and his overgrown beard stretching to his chest. His look kind of reminded me of a wizard. Then, I wondered if there really were wizards and if they would find that insulting.

"Eden, he's still here!" Ava shrieked.

"Who's here, Ava?" I said just as something solid crashed into the side of my head. The blow sent me to the floor on my side. Clutching the spot where I'd been kicked, I turned to meet the glowing eyes of Harper. He smirked down at me and took hold of one of my ankles, dragging me toward him.

"Eden!" My father's shaky voice groaned.

"Nija knew you would return, little Witch. She sent me here to make sure you don't go back and spoil her games. Paid good coin, too. What say you to that?" He twisted my ankle to flip me onto my back. My head banged against the floor and I heard Ava whimper near me.

"Leave her alone, you monster!" she cried. I would have

laughed if not for the pain in my head. That was my girl, my Ava. Even in the face of obvious danger, she would fight for me. My heart swelled as I understood that I would do the same. I would die for her, and my father if I must. A consciousness crept in, saying that death might come sooner than I had anticipated. Elevating my hands so that my fingers were all pointed at Harper, all I could think about was defending them.

"We gonna fight again, Witch? Don't you remember what happened last time?" Harper growled in amusement.

My power was stable inside of me, I could feel it steadily coursing through my veins. I thrust it into my fingertips as hard as I could, causing an explosion of light to erupt between Harper and myself. His deep voice filled the small house with a cry as I scrambled to my feet, easily pulling free of his grasp during the confusion. Not allowing him a moment to recover as the light faded, I took a step toward him, throwing a sphere of fire into his broad chest. I prepared to attack as it slammed into him, launching him into the wall.

With another step came another fireball, this one smashing into his face, making his glowing eyes disappear beneath his eyelids as he shut them for protection. My goal wasn't to kill, just to disable him so I could flee with my family. His rage was bleeding into me, though, I could feel my heart seething, ready to do whatever it took to make sure he didn't hurt the ones I loved. The air around my feet started to swirl as I let the flames take hold of the breeze, building a flaming storm around my body. I stepped to Harper, so close that I could touch him if I wanted.

His eyes jolted open, his mouth twisting into a hateful word as I released the strength of my spell onto him. I felt a small twinge of regret as my fire twister devoured him, pulling at him until he shattered into bits of ash. So much for fire not hurting a Demon, I thought. Holding my position, I watched as the spell died down and there was nothing but ashes drifting through the air. A rustling and the sound of heavy breathing behind me reminded me that I wasn't alone in the dwelling.

With a twist of my heel, I returned to Ava and my father. They were both gawking at me with wide eyes and gaping mouths.

"I'll explain later, for now, we need to get back to Rowan's castle," I said as I untied them.

"Now wait just a minute young lady. Who is Rowan and why does he have a castle?"

I laughed and pulled them both into my arms, tears running down my cheeks in relief. Letting myself momentarily forget that I had just killed someone, I allowed myself the comfort of my family's embrace.

"I've missed you guys so much," I said sincerely, placing a kiss on each of their foreheads. My father's was cold and clammy, I noticed. "I need you both to trust me, okay? I'm going to take you somewhere safe, somewhere--" I looked into my father's eyes that matched Ava's, feeling a twinge of sadness due to what I knew. "There are healers there, Dad. They can help you more than any mortal medicine."

"Mortal? Eden, you're talking funny." He said in a gruff voice, sending himself into a coughing fit. I wished that I knew how to harness the healing I'd done on myself after the Trial of Might. Patting my father on the back softly with one hand, I squeezed Ava's fingers with the other before standing up and grinning at them both.

"Watch this," I said and turned around, pulling the crystal from my dress and pulling through the air. Ava's gasp behind me was the only motivation that I needed to finish the symbol and whisper the word.

"*Brruntek.*"

As soon as the portal opened, I turned back to them, my hand outstretched. Ava's head shook slightly as she stared at the glowing, sparkling portal behind me.

"Just don't struggle against the damn thing," I said as their eyes darted between me and my magical gateway. "It will cause you to land on your ass."

"Watch your mouth," My father said, staring past me and into the opening.

"You can't be serious, Eden. What the fuck is going on? You just killed a guy." Ava cried. My father glanced at her, as though he were about to scold her for her language, too, but thought of something better. "And what are you wearing?"

"I'd have to agree with your sister, pumpkin. What the hell is happening here? Are you in some kind of trouble?" Oh no, I thought with a chuckle. He was going cop-mode on me. How could I explain to them that they guy wasn't really a guy, he was a sword-for-hire that had come to kill us all? Reasoning that magic had something to do with a gang, it was in his nature to question it.

"No, I'm not in trouble, dad. That was a Demon--" I held up my hand to stop their questions from forming. "It will be easier to explain when I can show you. And this would be a wedding dress," I motioned at the dress that was freshly dotted with soot. "We must hurry, or trouble might find its way back here. Now, come on." I yanked Ava up by her arm and started to push her toward the magical hole. My newfound strength helped me to edge her across the room.

"Why didn't you say that you were running off to get married?" She howled, struggling against me. Her stare swept across my dress again. "And to a rich guy, I see. That is--" she brushed her fingers over the diamonds, "if these things are real. They are real, aren't they?"

"Not just rich," I grinned and tousled her lovely hair that was once as red as my own. "He's a Prince."

Without giving her a chance to ask another question, I effortlessly shoved her into the opening before holding a hand out for my father. He stared at me in disbelief but grabbed my hand, allowing me to pull him up and drape his arm over my shoulders before walking the two of us through the portal. I clung to him as hard as I could without hurting him, until our feet thumped onto the ground in the castle courtyard. Ava was flat on her back, rubbing her head in the broad daylight of the Realm.

"I told you not to fight it, Ava. Now--" I breathed with a smile, pointing at the Keep. My father looked a little woozy but otherwise unscathed as his eyes met where I was motioning to. "Welcome to Lord Blaive's castle, in the Fae Realm."

Chapter Twenty-Seven

GUARDS HAD SURROUNDED US WITHIN SECONDS, TAKING EACH of us by the arms as though we had stabbed someone in front of them.

"We aren't gonna fight you," my father said, throwing his hands up and going full cop mode as they tore him from my grip. "No need to hurt anyone, alright?"

"Don't you recognize me?" I asked the guard, holding me as they began to move us toward the enormous entrance of the castle. "I'm Eden Morris, Princess to the Coven and winner of the Devotion Trials. I'm to be wed to Lord Blaive."

"You mean to say, 'His Majesty,'" the guard said gruffly, freezing in his tracks. With a motion to another guard, who took off into the castle, he stared at me for a moment while the others brought my family into a line behind me. How long had I been away? Rowan was meant to be crowned after we were married. I leave for a few hours, and all of a sudden, he is a King? Something didn't feel right.

"Be careful with my father," I said respectfully to the guard who was holding my arms tightly, most likely so I couldn't perform spells. Though, I was fairly certain, my arms wouldn't need to be raised to send a shock through his armor and onto his most intimate bits if I wanted to. "He is ill. Why are we just standing here in the hot sun anyway?"

"Ser Azrael will be arriving soon, to tell us if you are who you say. In the meantime, you will stand here in the scorching sun–" He glanced at my father with a scowl. Evidently, Rowan wasn't the only one who had received a new title in my absence. I felt a twinge of grief, combined with appreciation. Azrael deserved to be knighted, I wasn't going to argue with that. But it seemed like so much had changed already. "Illness" or no."

"You're an asshole," Ava said in a barely audible voice. Oh, how I had missed her. The guard holding her must-have tightened his grip, as she winced and fell silent. We stood to wait for what seemed like hours before the guard that had run off came back. He was in the company of Azrael, who was dressed in the same armor as the others but now sported a thick, midnight blue wrap over his wide shoulders. A knight *and* a captain of the guard. He was moving up in the world.

"Holy hot guy," Ava breathed. I glanced over my shoulder to see her smiling pleasantly at the tall newcomer. I didn't blame her for ogling. Azrael was gorgeous, with his tightly-twisted ropes of hair that were kept reasonably close to his scalp, but long enough to slope to one side. His body was constructed of sheer muscle, to the point that throwing a rock at him would probably damage the rock, not to mention his gleaming golden stare that matched the armor on his broad chest. "I'm Ava."

"Pleasure to meet you, Lady Avangeline," Azrael said in a rumbling voice, with a slight nod of his head in her direction. I was sure that his eyes lingered on her for a second or two longer than the rest of us, making me smother a smirk. He would be crazy not to find Ava attractive, as everyone else always had. He bowed his head to my father as well, before his dazzling gaze landed on me. "Lady Eden, welcome back. We did not think that you would be returning."

"Yeah, well, I'm here--" I struggled as the guard's hold on me tightened and looked at Azrael with a sigh. "Can you tell them to release us now? I am who I say, you know that."

"Thank you, men, that will be sufficient. Please, show Lady Eden's family to our guest wing and make sure they are assigned servants while I take the Lady to King Rowan." I gave my father and sister a reassuring nod as the guards went from intruder-mode to guest-mode.

"And a healer for my father, if you please."

"Indeed," Azrael nodded again to the guard holding my father. "Please see to it that his health is tended to by the healers, Fawks."

"Thank you."

I watched them enter the castle, following alongside Azrael. After ascending the stone steps, we parted ways with my family and headed to the northern wing. I still wasn't an expert in navigating the castle, but I knew the area to be where the throne room was. My stomach was in knots. What if Rowan became furious at my return? What if he sent me away and locked me out of the Fae Realm altogether?

"King Rowan has no right to keep you from this Realm. It is your birthright to be here, my Lady," Azrael said with a soft tone in his voice. Okay, that was disturbing. The first time he had done that, I figured it was just a lucky guess on his part. Now I was sure that he had mind-reading capabilities. That would make for a highly valuable Knight. Azrael chuckled before his face grew dark.

"What is it?" I asked, eyeing him carefully. The feeling in my gut that told me something was off started to come back.

"It is not my place to say, I'm afraid."

That was all that I could get out of him, and we spent the walk to the massive throne room entrance in silence. Frowning at the doors, I felt my fingers trembling at my sides as I waited to open them and, in turn, hear my fate. Azrael wrapped a hand around one of mine and gave it a quick squeeze before removing it and pushing one of the heavy doors open. Elevating my bowed head, I could see that Rowan rested on one of the glistening thrones at the opposite side of the room.

The chamber was a lot less daunting in the daylight hours, with sunlight pouring in through the tall, stained glass windows. Seafoam eyes locked onto mine, disbelief lying within them. My heart leaped into my throat as Azrael gave me a small nudge. *Put one foot in front of the other, just move.* I did as my mind commanded and began to walk the dark blue runner to the thrones. The closer I got, the more I started to realize that Rowan was not alone.

Beside him stood Nija and a group of other Demons, all of them sporting fancy, regal garb. Rowan's stare didn't waver as I approached, settling my feet just before the first stone steps leading to the platform where the others stood. I felt like a criminal, being tried for my crimes under the stares of the Demons. Nija had a wicked, half-smile on her face. I wasn't sure why she was so happy to see me, but I had a hunch that I wasn't going to like it.

"Your Grace." I curtsied to the best of my ability and then straightened, waiting for him to speak. His lips were slightly parted, his brows drawn as though he were trying to figure out if I was a hallucination. He cleared his throat and shifted in his seat, his eyes never breaking contact with mine. The tightness in my chest made it hard to breathe. I could see the light reflecting off of my ridiculously sparkly dress dance on my face as my breast heaved.

"Lady Eden, I did not expect your return, forgive me." Rowan raised from the throne, his sturdy golden crown gleaming atop his head in the daylight. Nija shifted her eyes from me to him as he moved to me, bowing his head. I have to admit, I was a little disappointed. All I wanted to do was throw my arms around his neck and kiss him until the moon rose in the sky-- My thoughts were cut off by Azrael shaking his head ever-so-slightly at my side.

Okay, guess that option was off the table. "Why have you come here?"

"To marry you, of course," I said simply, watching as the others stirred and released stifled laughter as though there was a joke floating around that I hadn't been involved in. "Your Highness," I added, not sure what was expected of me now that Rowan had been crowned as King. Nija's shrill laugh echoed throughout the hall, making my blood turn cold as she moved to Rowan's side and looked at me like I was a child eating mud. I looked at her gown, which resembled the one that she had worn at our first meeting. The thing barely covered her undesirables as she walked, and I was pretty sure that if she moved the wrong way she would bare it all to everyone.

"Shall you tell her, my King, or would you like for me to?" Rowan's shoulders tensed at her words, his eyes lowering in disgrace. I looked back and forth between them.

"Someone had better tell me!" I practically shouted. It wasn't the most graceful thing I'd ever done, but the feeling in my gut was becoming overwhelmingly filled with fear, the anticipation nipping at my backside. Rowan glanced up from beneath his thick lashes and looked at Nija with a single nod.

"Very well," She grinned wide enough to show all of her hideous, pointed teeth and stepped in front of him, blocking the King from my view. "Lady Eden, of the Coven, you are not eligible to wed his Majesty, as you did not win the Devotion Trials."

"What are you talking about?" I spat, my heart began to race. "You were bested, making me the last one standing. Well, sort of standing. Who are you to determine--"

Nija held up a hand to stop me and kept the wicked grin on her face as she lifted the other. My heart sank at the sight of what hung from her hand. The crystal flashed under the sun's beam, the silver chain sparkling as it swayed.

"How did you get that?"

With a sharp finger, she pointed behind me. I spun on my heel, my heart hammering in my chest as I observed Scott, who was advancing from behind. His blue gaze was locked onto mine, his head dropped, somewhat. Nija clutched my shoulder and whirled me around to face her again. Her face was so close to mine that I thought about spitting in it. Another head shake from beside me told me that would be a bad idea. I was at the mercy of the Demon.

"He can explain in further detail if he so chooses." She said, tilting her head. "You see, Eden, deception in the Trials is prohibited. You wore additional protection and, as I'm sure you know, that is against the rules of the game." Her voice was just above a whisper.

"And what of your cheating, Nija?" I snapped and took a step away from her, knowing that if I stayed that close, I would end up finishing what we had started in the colosseum. With a shrug, she twisted around and stepped back to the throne's side, allowing Rowan to look at me. A flash of light shimmered through his pale eyes. Why was he so quiet? "Rowan--King Rowan, that is--please, speak to me. What is she saying, exactly?"

"She has demanded a retrial, Eden. There is nothing I can say against it as the pair of you violated the law." He replied softly, turning around to retreat to his chair. I noticed his hands were tightly balled into fists as he left me standing there like an idiot, with my mouth hanging slightly agape. I glanced between the two, unsure of what was coming next.

"A retrial meaning--" I paused and struggled not to slap Scott across his face as he settled at my side. Rowan's eyes bore into the man like he still wanted to rip him to shreds. I took a step to the side, putting some distance between us. *How could he have told Nija? It wasn't even my idea to wear the stupid charm. Traitor. Swine.* I wished that Scott possessed Azrael's ability to read thoughts. I was more than prepared to give him a vigorous mental lashing.

"Exactly as it sounds, pretty little thing," One of the massive

Demons chimed in, stepping behind Nija and placing his hand on her shoulder. I sized the man up from head to toe. He looked like a male version of Nija but sporting a bit more clothing that happened to be the same color of dark, blood-red. "You will be obligated to, once again, prove your worth to ascend in the Royal food chain. A new set of Trials will begin promptly. This time, with proper precautions set in place."

"Yes," Nija chimed in when he had finished. "Your beloved King has agreed to our terms. In full, this time," She ran a finger-nail across Rowan's shoulder, and I swear that I saw him shiver. Sinking onto the arm of the throne, she brought her pouty lips right next to his pointed ear. "Isn't that correct, lover?"

I looked at Rowan with eyes that I'm sure exposed the hurt burning within me at Nija's use of the word.

He was a fucking King, for the love of Pete.

Why didn't he just find a scepter to slam against that pretty little throne of his and put a stop to the Demons and their nonsense? His eyes locked onto mine, and he gave me a twisted grin before looking up at his so-called lover.

"Not all of them, Nija," He said, regaining his tone of author-ity. "Not all of them."

Keep Reading!

Grab the next book in the series today!
All 3 books in this series are NOW Available!

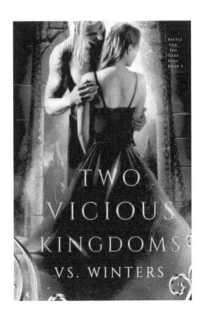

Join My Newsletter

Thanks for taking the time to read book! I really hope you enjoyed it. I'm already hard at work on more awesome books and I can't wait to share it with you.

In the meantime, be sure to sign up for my Newsletter so you can be the first to know about New Releases!
Subscribe Here!

About the Author

I write possessive, alpha heroes, and the women they can't live without! Sometimes... they start off as assholes...BUT I promise they'll melt your heart—along with your panties.

My favorite men are *Fae* but I also love a good demigod, vampire, shifter, warlock or demon! You'll notice every kind of hero in my books but the Fae hold my heart more than anything.

Subscribe to my newsletter to meet you next SUPER CRUSH! - Subscribe Here!

CPSIA information can be obtained
at www.ICGtesting.com
Printed in the USA
LVHW051156211021
701059LV00002B/38